MR AND MRS EVANS' HONEYMOON ON THE ISLAND OF MAJORCA, SPAIN

Michael Nwaduba

Grosvenor House
Publishing Limited

This book is published by
Grosvenor House Publishing Ltd
Link House
140 The Broadway, Tolworth, Surrey, KT6 7HT.
www.grosvenorhousepublishing.co.uk

NOTE:
This book is a work of fiction and some of the characters are fictitious
as well as some of the places mentioned. If any fictitious character resembles
anyone living, it's simply a coincidence, and the author is truly sorry for that.

Any use of the information in this book is entirely at the reader's
discretion and risk. The author or publisher cannot be held liable for
any loss, claim, or damage arising out of the use or misuse of the
suggestions made in this book.

Due to the dynamic nature of the internet, website addresses or links used in
this book may have changed since publication and may no longer be valid.
Hence, the author and publisher hereby disclaim any responsibility for them.

A CIP record for this book
is available from the British Library

ISBN 978-1-78623-409-4
eBook ISBN 978-1-80381-276-2

CONTENTS

HOW THE BOOK MR AND MRS EVANS' HONEYMOON ON THE ISLAND OF MAJORCA, SPAIN CAME TO BE

I never planned to write this book. Never! It was the book, *'Amazing Grace in Abundance'* I was writing when *'Mr and Mrs Evans' Honeymoon on the Island of Majorca, Spain'* manifested through divine power as an offshoot. Even when I resisted writing this book, it still came to be. I couldn't stop it.

On the 2nd of July 2017, at exactly 9 pm, the inspiration came, and I commenced writing *'Amazing Grace in Abundance'* not knowing what would happen in the future. After writing chapter 7 of the book, which is about the wedding of Mr and Mrs Evans, something new started developing and began to unfold. My initial plan was to write two or three paragraphs and annex it to chapter 7 as the honeymoon for the Evans'.

But God said to me, *"Separate it and do chapter eight as the honeymoon for the Evans'."*

I said, *"No, I can't do that. I have written a very good book up until this chapter 7. Why should I spoil it by writing on something people will consider as immoral? In any case, I don't even know what to write."*

I dropped my pen and paced around my living room and then sat down and began to reflect and meditate. I resisted writing chapter eight to the extent that I even considered getting rid of the couple Mr and Mrs Evans from the book, but the thought of it made me troubled because to do that would seriously distort the story. And then I remembered what happened to me when I wrote my first book – '*A Simple Guide for Bible Study.*' The Holy Spirit directed me to include a chapter in the book and I started arguing and did not obey. Immediately the flow of writing ceased and I couldn't write again. And I said, "*Lord, behold I can't write again. Why?*" He didn't say anything to me. And when I agreed to include the chapter in the book and obeyed, the flow of writing resumed, and I knew straight away, I wasn't even the one writing but the Holy Spirit just using me as a vessel to write.

To avoid a repeat of that incident, I immediately said, "*Lord I will write chapter 8 about Mr and Mrs Evans' honeymoon in Spain. I yield myself and my pen to you. I am not the one writing this chapter 8 but you are writing it using me as a vessel.*"

Immediately I said that, my head was flooded with ideas of what to write in chapter 8 of '*Amazing Grace in Abundance,*' and I went ahead and wrote it and I said, "*Whao! Maybe I should even write a book on this.*"

I read the chapter again and again, reviewed and screened it again and again and still nursed the fear that people will read the chapter and be offended and also see me as immoral. And I said, "*Lord, you are the one asking me to write this chapter 8, you will be the one to also defend me.*"

After writing the book '*Amazing Grace in Abundance,*' I gave the manuscript to a brother to review it for me, and he went straight and read and reviewed only chapter 8 of the book, Mr and Mrs Evans' Honeymoon. He didn't bother to read other parts of the book at all. Isn't it interesting to note that people including Christians like messages on the subject of romance, love, and sex? After reading chapter 8 of the book, he said to me, "*Is this what you call a honeymoon? My friend, I expect to see loads of romance, love and sex in this book, but I can't see that here. It is too shallow. Go deeper and tell us about the honeymoon the way it is as an author.*"

This comment was certainly a big relief to me after I have spent so much time worrying and beating myself up that what I had written was deep and may be seen as immoral. But most importantly, his comment now triggered the anointing in me; and I went ahead and wrote '*Mr and Mrs Evans Honeymoon on the Island of Majorca, Spain*' as a complete book. That's how this book was finally born. Isn't it interesting to note how this book finally manifested? – From, I will not write it, to I don't know what to write, to writing chapter 8, and then writing the book. What a process of gradual unfolding of this work! Today, I am glad I wrote this book. I pray this book will truly help to strengthen, revitalise, heal, and establish your marriage. Enjoy honeymoon every day of your life in Jesus' name. Amen!

MICHAEL NWADUBA

Chapter One: Day 1 – Sunday

The Island of Majorca, Spain

On Christmas Day in the city of Edinburgh, Scotland, Barry Evans and Priscilla Jenkins had their wedding before commencing their two-week honeymoon on the Island of Majorca, Spain. They arrived at Palma de Mallorca Airport in Majorca, Spain safely. As they went through the immigration checks they noticed that the officials were indeed friendly.

When they got to the counter, the immigration officer said, "My name is Leonardo. I hope you had a nice flight?"

They both answered, "Yes."

Leonardo now asked for their passports, and as he checked them he asked, "How long are you going to be with us in Spain?"

They said, "Two weeks."

He went ahead and stamped their passports and gave them back to them and said, "Enjoy your holiday."

They replied, "Gracias," meaning, "Thank you."

Leonardo answered and said, "De nada," meaning, "You are welcome."

Barry and Priscilla had earlier gone onto the internet to check out simple greetings and words in Spanish, and they were eager to try some out at the slightest opportunity.

As they walked out into the arrival lounge and beyond, they saw the beautiful lights, shops, and passengers arriving and departing to their various destinations in the busy airport. The airport is the third largest in Spain after Madrid, and Barcelona. They were immediately met by Antonio, the cab driver specially arranged by Champion 5-star hotel to pick them up. As he met them, he put on a smiling face and had a firm handshake with Barry and said in Spanish, "Mi nombre es Antonio de Champion Hotel." Meaning, "My name is Antonio from the Champion Hotel."

Barry answered, "Mi nombre es Barry y esta es mi esposa Priscilla." Meaning, "My name is Barry and this is my wife Priscilla."

Antonio said, "De nada."

They all got into the luxury *Mercedes-Benz S-Class* car and Antonio drove off heading for the Champion 5-star hotel on the seaside. They also have other nice hotels in Mallorca like Sheraton Mallorca Arabella Golf Hotel, Castillo Hotel Son Vida, and HM Martinique Aparthotel. The temperature has gone far below freezing point with heaps of snow and ice everywhere, hampering car access. As they arrived at the Champion Hotel, they alighted from the cab and went with their luggage to the reception for registration.

Champion is an exclusive hotel mainly for the bourgeois, tycoons, and celebrities. Barry specially chose it as a surprise for her. They both have positive surprises for each other that will take them over the moon on this once-in-a-lifetime honeymoon. At the reception they met a beautiful young Spanish girl full of smiles. She introduced herself to them as Nicole and asked in Spanish, "¿Cómo te llamas?" meaning, "What is your name?"

Barry answered and said, "Mr and Mrs Evans."

She quickly pulled up their files on the computer, asked for their passports for identification, while asking some other questions, completed their details and declared their registration complete, and gave them their suite details and keys.

It's Christmas Day, and while they were still at the reception, the popular Spanish Christmas carol song '*Feliz Navidad*'[1] meaning, 'Merry Christmas' or 'Happy Christmas,' by José Feliciano started playing.

As this song played, the vibrant newlywed pair began to sing, holding hands, and all eyes at the reception were fastened on them, but they seem not to notice because they were in their own world of honeymoon for two.

They proceeded to their lavishly furnished suite. Everything in this suite is massive, classy, and unique. The fantastic chandelier ceiling lights, decorations and artwork displayed on the walls caught her attention, and then the amenities. She stood still and started looking at each of the following beautiful paintings displayed on the wall: Les femmes D'Alger by *Pablo Picasso;* Mona Lisa by *Leonardo da Vinci;* and David's sculpture picture by *Michelangelo*. As she looked round, she had a feeling of joy and great satisfaction, and purred, "This suite is breathtakingly beautiful and I like it. You must have spent a fortune on this. Thank you sweetheart."

He answered and said, "You are welcome darling."

Once a couple is legally married, that gives them full licence to have sex. Sex is a very important aspect of a couple's marriage. Apart from the purpose of procreation, sex refreshes the soul. Have sex often, and if you've got the strength, do it daily. Whenever the word 'sex' is mentioned, some Christians frown at it as if it's a taboo to do so, and they do so perhaps out of pretext or ignorance. *Of what use is a honeymoon without talking about sex or having sex?* Many marriages are no longer exciting, and some others are as good as dead because romance, love, and constant sex have been excluded. Rekindle the fire in your marriage by engaging in serious romance, love, and sex. God created sex for married couples to enjoy. Therefore, enjoy it.

The Bible says in *1 Corinthians 7:1–5,*

1Now concerning the things whereof ye wrote unto me: It is good for a man not to touch a woman.

2Nevertheless, to avoid fornication, let every man have his own wife, and let every woman have her own husband.

3Let the husband render unto the wife due benevolence: and likewise also the wife unto the husband.

4The wife hath not power of her own body, but the husband: and likewise also the husband hath not power of his own body, but the wife.

5Defraud ye not one the other, except it be with consent for a time, that ye may give yourselves to fasting and prayer; and come together again, that Satan tempt you not for your incontinency.

Every married couple should look forward to a time to render due **benevolence** to their partner. And it's best to render it wholeheartedly, without reservations, being fully involved spirit, soul, and body in order to derive maximum satisfaction. It should be a time nothing else should matter to you in the world but you and the one you truly love. Verse 4 in the above scripture says you don't have full power over your own body anymore as your partner also has rights to it. Therefore, it's of no use denying your partner sex by making flimsy excuses. And the next verse reiterates this point by saying, "*Defraud ye not one the other...*" Create a fascinating honeymoon paradise world just for two of you.

Genesis 1:27-28 says,

> 27*So God created man in his own image, in the image of God created he him; male and female created he them.*

> 28*And God blessed them, and God said unto them, be fruitful, and multiply, and replenish the earth, and subdue it: and have dominion over the fish of the sea, and over the fowl of the air, and over every living thing that moveth upon the earth.*

According to the above scripture, God created Barry and Priscilla in His own image. And God blessed them for holy matrimony on Christmas Day saying, "*Be fruitful, and multiply, and replenish the earth,...*" How will a couple multiply and replenish the earth? By making love!

She gradually begins emptying their luggage and hanging their clothes in the wardrobe, and their shoes are neatly arranged in there. Barry has made a marriage vow to be a good husband to his wife, and turn over a new leaf, especially now that he has dumped Anna Murray. He calls out to her to come and join him for a short prayer and thanksgiving for the success of their wedding and safe arrival to Spain, and she joined him.

"Please turn off your mobile phone," says Barry, and both of them turn off their phones to avoid unnecessary disturbance from people calling and sending messages to congratulate them.

He starts praying, "Heavenly Father, we thank you for the success of our wedding, and smooth flight down to Majorca. Lord, we thank you for quenching the enemy's attack to spoil our marriage. It is by your mercy that we are joined together as husband and wife, and we appreciate your mercy. Lord, we thank you for all our guests. We ask that you protect all of them, and lead all of them safely back to their respective homes. Thank you Lord, for all the gifts we received from our family and friends, and we ask that you bless them more in Jesus' name." And they both say, "Amen!"

Immediately after the prayer, she held her husband and said, "I love you sweetheart. Thanks for everything."

He replies, "You are welcome."

He wanted to have a shower before making love, but her tender touch is irresistible. He held her firmly and, gazing at her face, they had eye contact, and she lowered her smiling face gently. She held his face close to herself and went straight for a kiss and they started panting with their eyes closed as they hurriedly begin to undress. He went straight for her bra and took it off exposing her moderate pointed succulent breasts. And they took the rest of their clothes off. He is determined to ensure that she reaches orgasm, so he started by gently fondling her and giving her a good massage, kisses, and fingering, to kick start her and get her wet before intercourse which sent both of them out of this planet, and they landed over the moon. What a honeymoon! She had earlier gone on the internet to explore new ways and styles of making love in order to reach orgasm, and also as a surprise for him.

Some of the new sex styles she discovered are, the Erotic Accordion, The Pinwheel, Electric Slide, X Marks the Spot, The X-Rated, Ladder Loving, Passion Propeller, Backstairs Boogy, Deep Impact, and the Bootyful View.[2] She concentrated more on the Bootyful View style because it allows for great control over speed, depth, and intensity of stimulation. She also tried the Jockey positions especially the straight one that allows her to be on top of Barry giving her full control to manoeuvre things the way she likes. As she tried some of these styles, Barry was absolutely dazzled. The beauty of trying some of these new styles is that most parts of the body are moved flexibly and it feels like exercising. In order to derive full pleasure and satisfaction from sex, it's vital to try a lot more styles, apart from the traditional missionary style and these styles should be tried in the bedroom, living room, bathroom, or wherever that is convenient. This gives the honeymoon variety, and makes it memorable.

She is also determined to satisfy him sexually if that will help permanently keep his attention away from Anna Murray or any other woman that may want to compete with her for her husband. They got together again to have carnal knowledge of each other and she participated fully by being involved spirit, soul, and body as she twisted her body flexibly, rather than just laying down like a log of wood and leaving him to do everything. She made very good romantic utterances which turned him on and helped him to be fully charged and energised with a lasting erection. Barry was indeed dazzled at her surprising new love-making techniques. It's soul-refreshing. Barry was quickened to remember the scripture below and he spoke it to her saying,

The Living Bible *(TLB)* says in *Song of Solomon 4:10-12,*

> [10] *How sweet is your love, my darling, my bride. How much better it is than mere wine. The perfume of your love is more fragrant than all the richest spices.*

> [11] *Your lips, my dear, are made of honey. Yes, honey and cream are under your tongue, and the scent of your garments is like the scent of the mountains and cedars of Lebanon.*

> [12] *My darling bride is like a private garden, a spring that no one else can have, a fountain of my own.*

These loving words from the Bible ignited more fire in her and she held him saying, "I love you darling. You are the sweetest. I'm all yours forever."

Barry replied, "I love you too honey."

She immediately positioned herself for the pretzel style which allows for deep penetration. And afterwards she also positioned herself in the cowgirl style, as well as the reverse cowgirl style, and they had intense sex until they were fatigued.

After making love, they headed straight for the Jacuzzi for a bath. Before their bath, they washed their teeth and tongue thoroughly to enhance dental care, fresh breath, and also make kissing more enjoyable. They washed one another's bodies while they laughed and shared jokes. "You are sweeter than honey my darling," says Barry and continued, "I enjoyed every bit of you. I like the way you held me tight and responded with kisses, and screams of approval, when we were making love. I hope you will do this to me forever?"

"Sure! I will even do much more," she replies. And that statement that she will even do more ignited another fire in him and he held her again in the massive Jacuzzi and they held each other tight and made love again.

As they carried out their fantastic love sessions, they had *Lionel Richie* love songs playing gently. When they finished in the bathroom, they put on their nightgowns and Priscilla sprayed a bit of her *Dolce & Gabbana Eau de Parfum*. Barry also sprayed a bit of his *Widian New York Eau de Parfum*. She went straight to him and put both arms around his neck with a little box containing a lovely birthday jewellery present she got for him and kissed him and said, "Happy birthday to you sweetheart. This special jewellery is for you." And he took the little box from her and held her tightly again and with their eyes closed, they engaged in a very soul-refreshing kiss and as they disengaged from holding each other he opened the box and found a golden *Gucci* bracelet, *Valentino Garavani* necklace, and *Rolex* wristwatch and he said, "Thanks a million for this. This is very much appreciated. I love you darling. I wish every day was a birthday for me so that I can get more presents from you."

Priscilla said, "You are welcome," and they started laughing. They got into the bed and under the thick quilt to keep warm while they held each other, kissed, and slept.

It's important to mention here that honeymoon is not just a western culture thing but that it's also biblical. The Bible says in **Deuteronomy 24:5** that, *"When a man hath taken a new wife, he shall not go out to war, neither shall he be charged with any business: but he shall be free at home one year, and shall cheer up his wife which he hath taken."* The Bible says here that a man should take one whole year off and be on honeymoon cheering up his new wife. And for a man to effectively cheer up his wife on a honeymoon there has to be loads of romance, love, and sex.

Chapter Two: Day 2 – Monday

Romance

It's Boxing Day and they woke up and did their morning devotion. They have already agreed that God will always be the head of their life and marriage. Therefore, they will always focus on Him, honour Him, and call upon Him for help and support. They started by singing praise and worship songs unto the Most High God, and then shared scriptures together. They recalled Rev. Dr. Lawrence N. Chukwuemeka's ministration the previous day at the wedding and read *Genesis 2:24*, *"Therefore shall a man leave his father and his mother, and shall cleave unto his wife: and they shall be one flesh."*

*"Once both of you are joined together in this union, you become one flesh. It's indeed a mystery established by the Most High God. And the union is meant to be until death, no divorce is permitted. A revelation of the fact that you are now one flesh means that you are not allowed to say or do anything that will hurt your partner, because you will indeed be hurting yourself if you do so. You are expected to do most things together. Sleep together, eat together, have fun together, and most importantly, your mode of communication has to change from singular to plural. For example, it has to be our, we, us, instead of I, me, and mine. It has to be **our** money, car, house, and not **my** money, car, or house.*

"The Bible says again in **Amos 3:3**, *'Can two walk together, except they be agreed?'*

"*Henceforth, you are expected to always be in agreement regarding your affairs. Quickly always agree together in matters affecting both of you. Do most things jointly in agreement including having a joint bank account, and joint mortgage – that's the spirit of oneness, unity, and absolute trust in marriage. Bear in mind that where there is agreement, there is always peace and progress. I would like to add here that there should be constant communication between both of you. Be quick to admit your faults, forgive one another, saying sorry when you ought to do so, and genuinely repent for your mistakes.*"

In the discussion that followed, they agreed that they will always do things together, and always be in agreement in line with the two scriptures above and the Man of God's ministration. After the discussion, Barry led her in a short prayer saying, "Father, we thank you for making it possible for us to be alive and well on this beautiful day. This is the day that the Lord has made, we will rejoice and be glad in it. We commit all our activities for the day to your hands as we ask that you guide and protect us. We thank you, Lord, for your Word that we shared this morning. We receive the grace to always be obedient to your Word, and also show respect for one another in Jesus' name. They both say, "Amen!"

After the devotion, they undressed to have a bath and are now completely naked. And as soon as they saw each other's nudity, they were fired up and Barry got a full erection and they were both in the mood for intercourse. He held her and began to kiss her and suck her breasts, and she was also responding, holding him tight as he penetrated and they became euphoric in the intense sex and she reached orgasm. They proceeded straight to the bathroom for a bath after the sex.

"That was brilliant," says Barry.

And pretending not to know what he was talking about she asked, "What was brilliant?"

Barry said, "I mean the sex."

Priscilla replied, "I want more."

"Are you Oliver Twist?" asked Barry, and they started laughing as she held him in the bathroom Jacuzzi, and positioned herself for another round of sex, which was much more intense than before as she was screaming out loudly, "Give it to me! Harder! More!"

Her screams energised Barry to do more until he was exhausted and they started to clean up. He now said, "I bet you are satisfied now."

"Not quite," Priscilla replied.

Barry said, "Well, we will get on with it later on."

"I'm just joking, I'm satisfied for now. You are fantastic!" Priscilla replied.

This put a smile on his face suggesting he is doing a good job.

They put on their love songs while they dress and afterwards, they walked down to the restaurant for breakfast which could have been brought to their suite, but they chose to walk down as it enabled them to see a bit of the hotel. They saw the beautiful plants, flowers, paintings, lighting and decorations of the hotel, which gave them a real sense of satisfaction, and for Barry, it showed that there is value for money paid.

When they got to the restaurant, they met a tall clean-shaven Spanish man who said, "Buenos dias, mi nombre es Juan Manuel. Por favor, ayudarse a sí mismo con todo lo que te gusta." Meaning, "Good morning, my name is Juan Manuel, please help yourself to whatever you like."

They replied, "Gracias."

They both went for cereal, and the complete English breakfast, consisting of bacon, sausages, scrambled eggs, tomatoes, mushrooms, and toast served on one plate for both of them. Barry got coffee, fresh orange juice, mango juice, and water. As they sat down, Barry cut out some of the scrambled eggs and fed her while rubbing her back gently and she responded saying, "Thanks honey."

He answered and said, "You are welcome sweetheart."

They continued with their meal while they briefly talked about the beautiful hotel and the excellent service they were getting. Barry gave her some sausage, and she said, "Thanks honey. The food is good."

"Yes, it's lovely. I'm enjoying it," replied Barry as he looked into her eyes and gave her a wink, and they smiled, and he stretched out his hands to reach out for her. He put his hands around her waist and she drew close to him as he gave her a peck on the cheek. After the food they sat back and relaxed fully while they watched the television and listened to the soft jazz music playing in the background. He spent time admiring his wife as he looks at her beautiful face, nicely styled hair, and the nice dress she wore.

He said, "Honey, you are beautiful and I love you."

To which she replied, "I love you too."

After a long while and a proper relaxation at the restaurant, they retired to their posh suite. When they got back he held her gently and said again, "You are so beautiful darling. You are my angel. I love you."

With a cheerful smile on her face Priscilla replied, "I love you too. You are simply the best."

He then held her more closely, fondling her succulent breasts and planting a sweet loving kiss on her, and that fired her up. Barry was aroused as he spoke to her of what the Bible says in *Proverbs 5:18-19,*

> [18]*Let thy fountain be blessed: and rejoice with the wife of thy youth.*

> [19]*Let her be as the loving hind and pleasant hoe: let her breasts satisfy thee at all times: and be thou ravished always with her love.*

The word '**ravish**' also means to *intoxicate* or *enrapture* as used in NKJV. He gently grabbed her breasts and continued to caress and kiss her and he became intoxicated with her love as they felt euphoric and then got into the mood to copulate, which was so intense, wildly emotional, and really satisfactory. They went into the bathroom to clean up, and came out and carried on listening to their favourite love songs. He brought out their chess game and they started playing. She used to be the champion in the past, but in a twist, he won the game that day and she joked and said, "I let you win because it is Boxing Day, and it was your birthday yesterday."

So he replied and asked, "What has all that got to do with my beating you darling?" She was silent.

He went to her and said, "You are so beautiful, and I love you."

"I love you too," replied Priscilla.

They got ready to go to the gym to work out and use the swimming pool. When they got to the gym within the Champion Hotel premises, they greeted the attendant saying, "Buenas tardes señor." Meaning, "Good afternoon sir."

The attendant replied, "Buenas tardes a usted," meaning, "Good afternoon to you." And he asked for her name and she said, "Priscilla Jenkins."

The attendant said, "No tengo Priscilla Jenkins aquí en el equipo. Lo que tengo es Priscilla Evans," meaning, "I haven't got Priscilla Jenkins here on the computer. What I've got is Priscilla Evans."

Barry said, "Please pardon her. You are right. It's for Mr and Mrs Evans. We just got married yesterday. I guess it hasn't sunk in well yet."

"I'm sorry sir. It hasn't registered well on the brain properly yet," said Priscilla, and that got all three of them laughing. They went past the entrance and got into the gym with their newly issued passes.

They started on the treadmills next to one another and started walking and then they increased the speed a little bit to moderate jogging, which they did for fifteen minutes and got off to use the recumbent exercise bike for another fifteen minutes. They went to do other light exercises for another fifteen minutes and left the gym for the swimming pool. They got into the swimming pool and noticed that the water was well heated, in spite of the chilly winter cold. Everywhere was also very clean. They stayed at the shallow end of the pool for a while holding one another tight and kissed before they dived in swimming. They stayed in the pool swimming for half an hour before they finally left for their suite.

They immediately got dressed in their smart clothes and left for the Champion Hotel restaurant and bar for some food and drinks. They ordered their food. Barry had always liked to have alcoholic red wine in the past, but Priscilla was surprised to see him order *Botonique* non-alcoholic Spanish red wine for both of them. She was thrilled because that was an indication of a new regime with a positive life changing lifestyle that will help their marriage. They both settled down on one of the beautiful upholstered sofas.

When their food and drinks arrived, they prayed and he fed her with some of the chicken breast and she said, "Thank you sweetheart," with a broad smile of approval. He leaned towards her and held her soft hand, squeezing it gently to feel her warmth. They concentrated on the food and he asked, "I hope you are having a good time so far on this honeymoon?"

She excitedly replied in the affirmative saying, "Of course sweetheart and I wish it would go on forever."

Barry said in a very gentle romantic tone, "I'm glad you are enjoying yourself."

They finished their meal, and he opened the non-alcoholic Spanish wine, and filled their glasses, and they held up their glasses and said, "Cheers!" together.

Barry sipped a little, and held her round her waist to bring her closer, and gave her to sip from his glass. Priscilla took a couple of sips and said, "This is a nice wine. I like it."

They had their wine and relaxed very well until she was feeling sleepy, resting her head on his side with her breast pressing tightly against him and he was stimulated and had a strong erection. And when he could no longer resist the erection, his thoughts focused on making love again, and he requested that they should return to their suite.

They immediately dashed out, and in a twinkle of an eye, they were back in their suite. He immediately held her and undressed her, unfastened her bra and other clothing, and they got together again digging it out and fabulously lost in love, as they headed again out of this planet to somewhere over the moon, perhaps landing on the stars. They made love energetically like crazy yet soul-satisfying and as they ended this session, she held him tight and whispered into his ears and said, "I enjoyed the sex. You are fantastic. I reached orgasm again and again on this honeymoon and I wish it could last forever."

Those complimentary words of approval set him on fire again as he got a full erection and they set off on another hot round of sex in this wild romance. As they ended this session, he saw tears of joy flowing ceaselessly down her cheeks. And she said again, "Honey, you are the sweetest. I'm all yours forever," and as she said this she remembered Anna Murray, Barry's ex-girlfriend, and with a cringed face she thought to herself, "If she ever dares to come near my husband again she is as good as dead, because she can't spoil my joy again." That was just an expression of a momentary surge of the emotion of jealousy. They went into the bathroom and had a bath in the Jacuzzi, dressed up in their night gowns, sprayed a bit of their perfumes, prayed, and got under the quilt, kissed and slept.

Chapter Three: Day 3 – Tuesday

What is love? & Cathedral de Mallorca

They woke up on the third day of their honeymoon which was going well so far, and they did their morning devotion. They sang praises unto the Lord, worshipped and adored Him, and prayed. They got into the Jacuzzi for a refreshing hot bath, and then dressed and went down to the restaurant for their breakfast. After they finished having their breakfast they came back to their suite. Meanwhile, their phones had remained off for most of the time, except when they occasionally switched them on and checked their messages.

As they came back, they decided to do Bible study on the subject:

WHAT IS LOVE?

The scripture below is taken from The New International Version (NIV) and gives a summary of what love is. Barry read *1 Corinthians 13:4-8 (NIV)* which says,

⁴Love is patient, love is kind. It does not envy, it does not boast, it is not proud.

⁵It does not dishonour others, it is not self-seeking, it is not easily angered, it keeps no record of wrongs.

⁶Love does not delight in evil but rejoices with the truth.

7It always protects, always trusts, always hopes, always perseveres.

8Love never fails. But where there are prophecies, they will cease; where there are tongues, they will be stilled; where there is knowledge, it will pass away.

TYPES OF LOVE

1. **Erotikos** is a Greek word. And it is the root word of the English word erotic. Erotic has to do with sexual passion or love. It is characterised by sexual desire. This is the kind of love that is so common in the world, and it is mainly of the flesh. This type of love does not last because it is mainly based on Sex! Sex!! Sex!!! Usually, people who engage in this kind of love don't have much connection with the things of God, and a condition may be attached to love. If you are in this kind of relationship, make the decision today to start rebuilding your love life based on the Word of God and not mainly on sex.

2. **Philanthropia** is also a Greek word. It is the origin of the English word philanthropy. This is love of mankind shown by practical kindness and help to humanity. We have charity organisations like the Red Cross giving this kind of love. We also have individual philanthropists who love mankind and give donations to worthy causes.

3. **Agape** is another Greek word. This is unselfish brotherly love. It is the unconditional love of Jesus Christ. This is the kind of love we ought to

express towards one another as Christians. Be mature in love to the point that the love of God is shed abroad in your heart by the Holy Ghost – Romans 5:5. Graciously shower your spouse with unconditional amazing abundance of love to help their soul refresh and keep prospering.

Their Bible study lasted just an hour but it gave them the opportunity to exchange views with an open heart and lovingly without any argument. Out of curiosity she asked Barry, "What type of love do we come under?"

Barry answered and said, "All three types of love are needed for a well-balanced and loving marriage. So we have to express all three types of love."

And she said again, "With all the sex we are having, I thought we come under erotikos only."

They both started laughing, and Barry answered and said, "But we are legally married and therefore licensed to have as much sex as we wish. Besides, we are sharing the Word of God to fortify us and our marriage."

She replied, "That's fine."

Afterwards, they got dressed and went out into the snow holding hands and chatting outside as they took a walk along the seaside, seeing the beautiful blue sky with the mild sun radiating down to the earth, and fish occasionally springing up from the waters and boats and ships passing through. They were outside playing and running along the edge of the great waters and having fun together as a few other tourists look on in admiration.

They moved on and boarded their special booked luxurious *Scania coach* to take them round the island of

Majorca for a sightseeing tour. As they got on, they greeted the tour guide saying, "Buenos días, señor." Meaning, "Good morning sir" and he answered and said, "Buenos dias, mi nombre es Lorenzo, y soy la guardia de tour para el día." Meaning, "Good morning, my name is Lorenzo, and I am your tour guide for the day." They settled on the coach, and the tour guide was on board to show them important landmarks in the city and environs of the beautiful island. They drove off and went to see the glorious Cathedral de Mallorca where they took photographs with their camera and mobile phones.

When they got there, the tour guide gave them information about the *Cathedral de Mallorca* saying, "This is one of the most exciting tourist attractions. It is 121 metres long, 55 metres wide, and its nave is 44 metres tall, and it sits on 6,600 constructed square metres of land, with a capacity for 18,000 people. The building of the Cathedral was started in 1229 by King James 1 of Aragon but finished in 1601. It was designed by famous Catalan architect Antonio Gaudin in the Catalan Gothic style but also has Northern European influences. It was built of sandstone blocks or ashlars. The cathedral is a magnificent piece of art considered to be the fourth most beautiful church in the world."[3]

They spent a while looking at the exterior artworks and beautiful design of the building. They posed and took pictures at strategic points of their choice, including the entrance. There were also other tourists there looking round this great building. After viewing the exterior, they finally went inside the cathedral. Behold, it's a massive auditorium, the building is very high and supported by huge pillars. The walls had various kinds of artwork with well-decorated superb lighting. They took pictures at different points.

While they were in the cathedral, one couple approached them and said, "Hello, congratulations to you two for your wedding."

They both replied, "Thank you."

Barry said, "Sorry, I don't think I have met you before."

The man answered and said, "We were at your wedding in Edinburgh. My name is Winston and this is my wife, Deborah."

Barry said, "It's a pleasure meeting you. My name is Barry, and this is my wife Priscilla. We are here for our honeymoon."

They all shook hands and embraced one another and carried on with their sightseeing.

"What a mismatch!" commented Priscilla about their height as they are a good distance apart. Winston is exactly five feet tall, and Deborah is five feet ten inches and very beautiful. She continued and said, "Could it be that he used charm on her to get her to fall in love?"

Barry replied, "Money is the charm. Once you have plenty of money, you can convince any woman out there."

Priscilla says, "Really?"

"Of course yes! If I don't have as much money as I do, you would probably not marry me," replied Barry.

She grabbed him from behind and they started laughing and some tourists started looking in their direction in admiration as they closed up and started kissing, forgetting they are in a holy place, not knowing if such behaviour is allowed there. And when she realised that she said, "We are inside a church. Let's behave."

When they finished their tour of the beautiful Cathedral, they got back on the coach and cruised through seeing the handwork of God embedded in nature, now being unraveled as a result of this great adventure called honeymoon. It's indeed exciting and the memory will forever live with them. Barry held Priscilla gently close to himself and put his hands around her soft waist and reached for her lips and they close their eyes as the tender kiss started pulling some chords in their nerves, sending a message of copulation to the brain to satisfy the soul. When they got back to Champion Hotel, they went straight to the restaurant and bar to have their meal, after which they went to their suite to relax.

After relaxing for a while, they got out their scrabble game and started playing. Barry used to be the winner in the past but on this occasion Priscilla won. And he said, "I let you win because it will be boring for me to keep beating you," and she quipped, "Really? Men and their ego," and she went close to him and held him from behind resting her breasts on him and said, "I love you sweetheart."

He felt a transmission of a love current from her into his calm body and he replied with a deep emotion of love, "I love you too," and turning round to see her beautiful face, he said again, "I have a poem from the Bible written by King Solomon I would like to read to you honey."

Priscilla said, "Please read it to me. I need the Word of God to thrill me more."

They opened to the Song of Solomon of The Living Bible Chapter four and he read verses one to seven to her in a romantic tone.

The Living Bible (TLB) says in **Song of Solomon 4:1-7,**

King Solomon:

> *¹How beautiful you are, my love, how beautiful! Your eyes are those of doves. Your hair falls across your face like flocks of goats that frisk across the slopes of Gilead.*

> *²Your teeth are white as sheep's wool, newly shorn and washed; perfectly matched, without one missing.*

> *³Your lips are like a thread of scarlet – and how beautiful your mouth. Your cheeks are matched loveliness behind your locks.*

> *⁴Your neck is stately as the tower of David, jewelled with a thousand heroes' shields.*

> *⁵Your breasts are like twin fawns of a gazelle, feeding among the lilies.*

> *⁶Until the morning dawns and the shadows flee away, I will go to the mountain of myrrh and to the hill of frankincense.*

> *⁷You are so beautiful, my love, in every part of you.*

When he finished reading it, she said, "Thanks Love, you have made me wet again!" and grabbed him firmly close to herself and planted her lips on him and said, "I love you."

Barry responded, "I love you too darling." The kissing went on for a long while, as they closed their eyes and caressed one another. They hastily begin to undress. And she immediately positioned herself in the missionary style as they became intoxicated in love. She could not hold herself and she began to scream out excitedly, "I love you sweetheart. You are fantastic. More! Harder!"

As they finished this exhilarating intense sex session, they went into the bathroom and had a bath. They romantically washed each other's bodies. They left the bathroom and put on their nightwear and sprayed their perfumes before sitting down together on their sofa. They watched the television and talked about the beautiful Cathedral they saw during the day. She rested her head on his side while he was busy fondling and kissing her. She grabbed his penis and said, "Oh my God, you've got a full erection already."

"Yes oh! That shows I'm alive," said Barry.

They started laughing as they stood up, turned off the television, and retired to bed. They held one another and kissed each other and slept.

Chapter Four: Day 4 – Wednesday

How to care for the penis and vulva; & Titanic

They woke up in the morning feeling very refreshed and started their morning devotion together, singing praises unto the Most High God and afterwards she prayed and Barry rounded up the prayers. They proceeded to do Bible study and Barry decided to share the Word of God on the topic:

WHY DO WE HAVE TO STUDY THE BIBLE?

This topic is very important because any marriage that will remain strong and healthy must be built with the Word of God. No shortcuts. We have to study the Bible as Christians for the following reasons:

1. *TO BOOST OUR FAITH:* The Bible says in **Romans 10:17**, *"So then faith cometh by hearing, and hearing by the word of God."* Continuous Bible study, whereby we spend quality time both *studying* and *meditating* on the Word of God will certainly boost our faith as Christians.
2. *TO RENEW OUR MIND:* Every Christian continually needs to renew their mind with the Word of God. The scriptures have the ability to renew polluted minds, and enable us continually

have the mind of Christ as we continue studying the Word of God. The Bible says in **Romans 12:2**, *"And be not conformed to this world: but be ye transformed by the renewing of your mind, that ye may prove what is that good, and acceptable, and perfect, will of God."*

3. **THE WORD OF GOD IS A PRAYER TOOL**: The only way you can effectively pray with understanding and not pray amiss is to pray using the Word of God, except you decide to pray in tongues. Praying without the Word of God is simply blabbing, and such prayers are impotent lacking the power of God to produce desired results. The Bible says in **Hosea 14:2**, *"Take with you words, and turn to the LORD."* From where will you take words? – The Bible.

4. **THE BIBLE CARRIES THE POWER OF GOD**: The Bible as letters or logos may be seen as powerless, but when you study and meditate on it and speak it out, it turns out to be a powerful Rhema word. **Hebrew 4:12** says, *"For the word of God is quick, and powerful, and sharper than any two edged sword, piercing to even the dividing asunder of soul and spirit, and of the joints and marrow, and is a discerner of the thoughts and intents of the heart."*

5. **THE WORD OF GOD BRINGS FORTH HEALING AND GOOD HEALTH**: **Psalm 107:20** says, *"He sent his word, and healed them, and delivered them from their destructions."* The way you receive the Word of God determines the extent it will bless you. If you exalt the Word of God maximally in your life, and see it as medicinal, it

will obviously heal you, and also deliver you from bondage when you receive it. On the other hand, if anyone despises the Word of God, it will not profit them anything. The Word of God is very powerful. It carries healing anointing in it. The Bible says in **Matthew 8:16** that, "*When the even was come, they brought unto him many that were possessed with devils: and he cast out the spirits with his word, and healed all that were sick.*" How did Jesus cast out the evil spirits, and heal all that were sick? –With His word. There was no anointing oil, or laying of hands. **Proverbs 4: 20-22** also says,

20My son, attend to my words; incline thine ear unto my sayings.

21Let them not depart from thine eyes; keep them in the midst of thine heart.

22For they are life unto those that find them, and health to all their flesh.

King Solomon clearly stated in the above scriptures that as we study the Word of God, and hold them in the midst of our heart, it will bring forth divine health unto all our flesh. This again proves that the Word of God heals.

After he finished delivering the Word of God, she said, "Thank you darling. I enjoyed your teaching. From the way you are going, I won't be surprised if you become a Pastor one day in future."

They both started laughing as he said, "God has not called me into that office. If He calls me, I will take up the job. I will not try to run away like Prophet Jonah." As he said that, they started laughing out loud again.

"Honey, I have a question to ask you regarding today's teaching," said Priscilla. "Apart from hearing the Word of God to boost our faith according to Romans 10:17, are there other things we can do to boost our faith?"

Barry replied and said, "Good question. Some of the synonyms of faith are trust, belief, confidence, and reliance. Apart from studying and meditating on the Word of God, having full trust, belief, confidence, and reliance on the Word of God can also boost your faith. Avoid all doubts; this can be done through practicing what you study in the Bible with all boldness. I have to mention here that your faith can also be boosted when you read other materials apart from the Bible that will edify you. Choose such materials wisely as you are led by the Holy Spirit."

Thank you very much sweetheart for your further explanation," Priscilla replied.

Barry said, "You are welcome darling."

She turned on the television, while they start undressing to have a bath. They got into the Jacuzzi and romantically held one another and washed one another. They finished and came out and dressed up ready for breakfast in the restaurant, they entered the restaurant they met a beautiful lady and they said, "Buenos días."

The lady stopped and said, "Buenos dias, mi nombre es Lucia. Por favor, ayudarse a sí mismo con todo lo que te gusta." Meaning, "Good morning, my name is Lucia. Please help yourself with whatever you like." They went ahead and served themselves English breakfast consisting of baked beans, bacon, sausages, mushrooms, tomatoes, and toast. They also got porridge, tea, mango juice, pineapple juice, and water.

When they finished eating they relaxed and went back to their suite. They decided to check their mobile phones and discovered that they now have loads of text messages, emails, WhatsApp, Facebook messenger messages, and missed calls. They had to spend a while replying to the messages and returning a few calls from friends and family. They now got ready to visit the Royal Palace of La Almudaina. They left the hotel and climbed into their booked coach and their tour guide was on board to show them around.

When they got there, the tour guide started giving them information about the Palace saying, *"The Royal Palace of La Almudaina,* meaning, 'Palacio Real de La Almudaina,' is the Alcázar (fortified Palace) of Palma, the capital city of the Island of Majorca, Spain.

The construction of the Palace commenced 1281 and it is the home to the King and Queen. The building has a rectangular tower comprising home for the King and Queen, Tinell Hall, the Royal chapel, and patios. La Almudaina Palace was the seat of the independent kingdom of Majorca during the reigns of King James 1, Sancho 1 and James 11, until it became part of the kingdom of Aragón under Pedro IV. It stands opposite Palma Cathedral with commanding views over the Bay of Palma.

The palace is owned by the Spanish government and operated by Patrimonio Nacional, an agency of the Minister of the Presidency that manages assets of the

State for the Crown. Nowadays, the Royal Family uses it as an official residence for ceremonies and State receptions, having their private summer residence in the Palace of Marivent on the outskirts of Palma.

The Palace is open to the public for viewing as a tourist attraction from Tuesday to Sunday plus public holidays from morning to evening."[4-5]

They followed the tour guide as he conducted them round the different rooms of this great palace. They saw the thick walls and art decorations of the fortified Palace along with the unique furniture. There were also other tourists in the Palace viewing this magnificent edifice.

Afterwards, they came back to their suite and Barry got out his *Epiphone Acoustic* guitar and started playing for her this beautiful song:

Priscilla my love
There is none like you
In the whole wide world
You are so beautiful
You are so lovely
I'm glad to have you in my life
You make me feel like this
Honeymoon should last forever
I will never let you go

Oh! Oh! Oh!
Priscilla my love
Please let me hold you close to me forever
Let me kiss you forever
I dream of you

I visualise our honeymoon memories every minute
It's going to last forever with me
Priscilla my love
You are sweeter than honey
And I will always love you
Thank you for being my wife

As he played the strings of the guitar and sang those beautiful lines to her, she gazed at him in amazement with a heart overflowing with joy, and tears of joy ran down her tender cheeks. As he put down the guitar she grabbed him and said, "I love you honey. I love that beautiful song." She went straight for a kiss and she was now in the mood to make love.

He said, "You are welcome."

They started undressing and he grabbed her succulent breasts and started sucking them and that got her wet and he carried on kissing, massaging, and fingering her. She held his penis and gently rubbed it down and positioned herself for Barry to penetrate her from behind in a Man's best friend style, Alias Doggy style. This position allows for deep penetration allowing the penis to touch the cervix and also a good view. This sex session was very intense as he had a full erection. And as they finish they went into the bathroom to have a bath.

And she asked Barry, "I see that you have full erection, and you are very active during sex. How do you care for your penis in order to keep it very active?"

Barry answered and said, "I care for my penis in a number of ways in order to keep it healthy and active. I do the following:

HOW TO CARE FOR THE PENIS

1. Wash the penis and the scrotal sack daily, gently with warm water.
2. Wear underwear once daily and make sure it's not too tight to allow some air flow, preferably boxer shorts.
3. Ensure you keep your pubic hair short so that it will not serve as a breeding ground for boils, rashes, or any kind of infection or disease.
4. Report any unusual swelling of the scrotum, rashes, or infection to the doctor immediately.
5. Eat more fruits, vegetables, and proteins, nutritious food that will help keep the sperm healthy.
6. Eliminate the use of tobacco, as it causes cancer and reduces the supply of oxygen in the body.
7. Consume no alcohol.
8. Sleep well. Have about six to eight hours of sleep daily.
9. Have regular exercise to help cut down on the belly and it also helps free flow of blood through the arteries.
10. Reduce stress which causes the release of adrenaline hormones, which in turn narrows blood vessels.
11. Have sex regularly to keep the urinary and sperm track free and keep the penis active.
12. Go for regular check-ups for prostate cancer.[6]

As you do all these the penis will remain active and healthy."

She said, "Well done. I like your answer."

"How do you care for your vagina?" Barry asked, and she answered and said, "I care for my vagina in the following ways:

HOW TO CARE FOR THE VULVA

1. Wash the vulva with warm water daily.
2. Avoid using douches except when prescribed by the doctor.
3. Dry the vulva with a clean towel.
4. Wear 100 percent cotton underwear and avoid other fibres.
5. Avoid wearing thongs.
6. Wash new underwear before wearing.
7. Always keep the pubic hairs short so that it will not serve as a breeding ground for rashes, boils, or infections. This will also avoid pubic hairs getting into the vagina to hurt during sex.
8. Avoid using public toilets if you can.
9. Use tampons or pads instead of sanitary napkins to control menstrual bleeding.
10. Avoid scratching.
11. Report any rashes, boils, or unusual swelling or bleeding to your doctor immediately.[7]

When she finished, Barry said, "That's a good answer. I'm glad you take good care of yourself. Good personal hygiene helps intercourse, and keeps us healthy."

Priscilla replied and said, "Thanks darling." They dressed and went to the restaurant to have their lunch. They served themselves potatoes, chicken, mixed vegetables and gravy. They also got fresh apple, banana, mango and orange juice, plus water. As they settled down and ate the food, Barry said, "I need to fuel up properly because I have burnt a lot of energy."

"What have you done?" Priscilla asked.

"Making love. It drains a man's strength," Barry replied.

She laughed and said, "That means I am satisfying you well."

And he answered and said, "You are indeed satisfying me."

They both started laughing as he drew her close to himself and gave her a kiss, and she said, "Thank you darling."

When they came back to the suite, they settled down to see a romantic movie. They have a number of romantic movies lined up to see during this honeymoon.

"Honey, which romantic movie shall we see?" she asked him.

"Can we watch Titanic?" Barry answered.

"Great! I had that in mind too," said Priscilla.

She pulled the film from the internet and they settled down to watch the exciting romantic movie. Priscilla opened a bottle of *Chateau de Fleur* non-alcoholic sparkling American wine and filled up two glasses and they lifted up their glasses and said together, "Cheers!"

And Priscilla said, "*Titanic* is a 1997 American epic romance movie based on a fiction story of a poor artist called Jack Dawson (Leonardo DiCaprio) and a rich girl called Rose DeWitt Bukator (Kate Winslet) who fell in love on the great ship. This was the first and only trip of the great ship called RMS Titanic, a British passenger liner. The ship was described as unsinkable, and it set sail from Southampton on 10th April 1912 heading for New York City. Unfortunately, the ship collided with an iceberg on the 14th of April, 1912 and sank the next day at about 2.20am in the North Atlantic Ocean. Only 705 people survived the shipwreck out of over 2,000 people who were on the ship. The film was directed, written, co-produced and co-edited by James Cameron.

Rose was on board the ship with her fiancé Caledon Hockley, but hooked up with Jack in the cruise romance. When the ship collided with the iceberg, there was so much commotion in the ship as the water gradually began to fill the great ship, until it was greatly ripped apart and water began to gush in seriously and all through, Rose and Jack held on to one another in a love tie. Eventually, seven hundred and five people were saved in lifeboats including Rose, while Jack died. And eighty-four years later, at the age of one hundred, Rose tells the story about her life on the Titanic to her granddaughter and friends, and her romance with Jack and struggle for survival when the ship had the accident and began to sink."[8]

As they watched the film, Priscilla became so emotional and was in tears and Barry said to her, "That's alright darling. It's only a film. You don't need to be deeply emotional to be in tears."

Priscilla replied saying, "The devastation on this great ship is much, and it has claimed a lot of lives, shattering the romantic affair of Rose and Jack." She quoted *Song of Solomon 8:7*, "*Many waters cannot quench love, neither can the floods drown it: if a man would give all the substance of his house for love, it would utterly be contemned.*"

Barry said, "Amen! Our love will remain strong forever in Jesus' name," and they both said, "Amen!"

They continued to share their views and scenes of interest in this great film. They put on their music playing love songs and sat on the sofa in front of the television caressing one another. After a while, they decided to dress and go down to the restaurant and have their dinner.

When they got to the restaurant, they met Andrea and greeted her saying, "Buenas noches." Meaning "Good evening" and she answered and said, "Buenas noches."

They went ahead and served themselves mashed potatoes, fish, mixed vegetables, gravy, salads, and assorted fruits. They also got French white non-alcoholic champagne which they really enjoyed. After much relaxation, they went back to their suite and got into their night gowns and retired to bed with a good night kiss and went to sleep.

Priscilla got up in the early hours of the morning to use the toilet. And after that, she held him and started massaging him, holding his penis and that woke him up and aroused him to have a full erection and they got together and made love before going back to sleep again.

Chapter Five: Day 5 – Thursday

Why do we have to study the Bible?
& Romeo and Juliet

They woke up in the morning feeling so refreshed. They did their morning devotion together singing praises unto the Most High God and afterwards she prayed and Barry rounded up the prayers. They proceeded to do Bible study and Barry continued on the same topic from the previous day's ministration to share the Word of God and the topic is:

WHY DO WE HAVE TO STUDY THE BIBLE?

This topic is very important to them because they have decided that they will make the Word of God the basis and standard for their marriage and life. They will make all decisions based on what the Bible says and apply it to their way of life. If an argument ever arises, the Word of God will be the final umpire. That's how serious and valuable they hold the Word of God. They hold it in high esteem. When we know why we have to do something which, essentially, are the benefits, it does serve as a motivation for us to do it. We have to study the Bible as Christians for the following reasons:

1. *STUDYING THE BIBLE WILL MAKE GOD APPROVE US.* The Bible says in *2 Timothy 2:15,*

"*Study to shew thyself approved unto God, a workman that needeth not to be ashamed, rightly dividing the word of truth.*" A thorough knowledge of the Bible causes us to be approved vessels of honour unto the Lord. God is pleased with people who are thoroughly furnished with His Word, having developed skills to interpret scriptures, as well as its application to their lives. The ability to compare scripture with scripture comes forth from studying. As we study the Bible, we also gain understanding and this helps us to rightly divide the word of truth. When we are able to do this, we are paving the way for God to use us as approved vessels.

2. **TO AVOID CAPTIVITY AND DESTRUCTION:** *Proverbs 10:14* says, "*Wise men lay up knowledge.*" Knowledge is a source of strength. King Solomon says again in *Proverbs 24:5,* "*A wise man is strong: Yea, a man of knowledge increaseth strength.*" The facts you have about a subject can save you from terrible situations. Lack of knowledge of a matter is synonymous to being in darkness. But light shines forth when adequate knowledge is in place. The knowledge to be acquired should not be limited to Bible knowledge only. Knowledge about other things in life is also essential as it also helps us make important decisions in life. The prophet *Isaiah* likens lack of knowledge to being in captivity when he said in *chapter 5:13* of his book, "*Therefore my people are gone into captivity, because they have no knowledge: and their honourable men are famished, and their multitude dried up with thirst.*" That is how terrible things can be for anyone who does not

hunger to have general knowledge of things, and in particular, knowledge of the Word of God. King Solomon writes in **Proverbs 19:2**, *"Also, that the soul be without knowledge, it is not good." **Hosea 4:6*** says, *"My people are destroyed for lack of knowledge: because thou hast rejected knowledge, I will also reject thee, that thou shalt be no priest to me: seeing thou hast forgotten the law of thy God, I will also forget thy children."* The Word of God makes it clear here that lack of knowledge will lead to destruction. The only way to avoid this happening is to reach out for your Bible, and start searching it to know what God is saying about your situation, and apply the scriptures to your life.

3. **TO AVOID MAKING MISTAKES:** Jesus said to the Sadducees, in **Matthew 22:29**, *"Ye do err, not knowing the scriptures, nor the power of God."* Jesus is simply saying here that those who do not study their Bible make mistakes, and they do not know the power of God either. It is a shame for anyone to choose to live their life making errors. That will only retard the person. Studying the Bible will help us know the power of God, and also make fewer mistakes in life. Let us look at what Jesus said to the Pharisees when they made silly comments about His disciples in Matthew chapter 12 as they plucked and ate ears of corn because they were hungry. Jesus said to the Pharisees in **Matthew 12:3 & 5**, *"Have you not read in the law...?"* Meaning, you people ought to have read or studied your Bible before now and know what the right answer should be regarding this matter. But they did not, so they ended up challenging Jesus' disciples.

4. *THE WORD OF GOD IS PROFITABLE FOR TEACHING AND CORRECTION: 2 Timothy 3:16-17* says,

16All scripture is given by inspiration of God, and is profitable for doctrine, for reproof, for correction, for instruction in righteousness.

17That the man of God may be perfect, thoroughly furnished unto all good works.

The Bible is authentic. It is also a book of authority. You cannot fault it the way other books are faulted because it has been tried like silver in a furnace of the earth, purified seven times and found to be pure, and therefore, a valuable tool for teaching and correction. The above scripture confirms that the Bible was written by men inspired by God.

5. *JESUS OUR ROLE MODEL STUDIED THE BIBLE*: As Christians, Jesus remains our number one role model. Hence, we have to continually follow His example. There is evidence, in the Bible that Jesus read His Bible. Now, if Jesus, our role model, read His Bible, then we have to emulate Him and read ours.

In *Matthew 4:4, 7 & 10,* Jesus wrecked the devil big time by quoting the scriptures to the devil three times saying, *"It is written."* For Jesus to quote the scriptures shows He has read them because you can only quote what you have studied.

The Bible also says in *Luke 4:16-17* that Jesus went to Nazareth where He was brought up and went into the synagogue and read the Bible as His custom was. This means that it was Jesus' practice to always go to the synagogue to read the Bible.

When he finished delivering the teaching, Priscilla said, "Thank you very much honey for that great teaching on why we have to study the Bible."

"You are welcome darling," said Barry.

Priscilla continued and said, "I have a question to ask, and the question is, why is it that some Christians don't practice what the Bible says?"

Barry answered and said, "Some Christians don't practice what the Bible says possibly because of the following reasons: *firstly,* some Christians don't even study their Bible, so they don't have knowledge of what to practice. *Secondly*, some Christians don't fully believe or trust what they study in the Bible. *Thirdly*, they see the standard of the Bible as too high for them to practice. *Fourthly*, there is no instant penalty for those who don't practice what the Bible says."

With a broad smile on her face she came close to him and said, "Excellent answer honey. Thank you very much. More wisdom and anointing upon your life honey."

He replied saying, "You are welcome darling."

As they finished their Bible study, they got ready to go to the gym and exercise. They got there and went straight to the treadmill and ran for thirty minutes to warm up. This cardiovascular exercise is very good for the heart as it helps the free flow of blood to and from the heart via the arteries and veins. They got off from the treadmills and went straight for the table tennis. She is very good at the game and she is the champion. Barry has been stepping up his game, but he is still not a match for her. They got their bats and commenced warming up. Her backhand and smashing are too hot for Barry, and it makes him nervous. As they warm up she sent across the unexpected backhands, and smashes, and Barry is already scared of playing officially with her.

After a while, she said, "Can we now start an official game, and do the scoring?" And he said, "Is there really any need for that? Let's carry on warming up in a friendly game." But she insisted on doing it officially and doing the scoring. They started the official game and got more serious. She started blasting him with hot shots and tricks which got him running up and down the standing area. As the game continued, Barry fired some surprising shots which got her to be more serious. She dominated most parts of the games and ended up winning the three games. Priscilla is the champion.

They got ready and left for their suite to have a bath. After the bath, they got dressed and went to the restaurant for breakfast. While they had their breakfast, he said, "You are a great tennis champion. Well done darling."

"Thanks for the compliment," she replied.

Barry continued, "I look forward to when I will start beating you." And they burst into laughter. They finished their meal and had some rest and went back to their suite.

When they got back to the suite, they put on the television, and their love songs played in the background. "What film are we seeing today honey?" he asked.

"Can we see Romeo and Juliet?" she replied.

"That's absolutely fine," said Barry.

She went ahead and pulled the movie off the internet and they settled down to see the sensational film. She got out one bottle of *Botonique* non-alcoholic Spanish wine and two glasses and served while they raised their glasses and said, "Cheers!"

Barry said, "Thanks for the wine." And they continue to watch the film.

Priscilla had read the book before, so she began to tell the story saying, "*Romeo and Juliet* is one of William Shakespeare's dramas written between 1591 and 1597. The play is set in the cities of Verona and Mantua, although most part of the play happened in Verona where the Montagues and Capulets live. In Act V, Scene 1, Romeo kills Tybalt and is banished from Mantua.

The noble families of the Montagues and the Capulets live in the city of Verona. They had an argument, and were enemies. Their servants were enemies as well. The young men who work for the Montagues and the Capulets get into gangs and fight each other in the street, because it is fashionable to carry a sword. Sometimes, they get badly injured.

Verona is ruled by Prince Escalus. He tells the Montagues and the Capulets that they have to stop fighting or they will be punished. It is very difficult to control the young men. Montague had only one child, a teenage boy called Romeo. Capulet also had only one child, a beautiful 14-year-old daughter called Juliet. They do not know each other, because Juliet never goes anywhere without her nursemaid. Romeo and his friends go to a masked ball at the home of Juliet's parents. Romeo and Juliet met at a party and fell in love.

Romeo and Juliet tried to hide their love affair at home by not talking about it because they think they will get into trouble with their parents. Juliet knows that her parents wanted her to marry a cousin of the prince. Romeo and Juliet get married in secret, and because of their secret marriage, a lot of things happened which brought about many deaths, including, Romeo and Juliet killing themselves.

In Romeo and Juliet, Shakespeare creates a world of violence and generational conflict in which two young people fall in love and die because of that love. The story is rather extraordinary in that the normal problems faced by young lovers are presented very big here. It is not simply that the families of Romeo and Juliet disapprove of the lover's affection for each other, but rather, the Montagues and the Capulets are on opposite sides in a blood feud and are trying to kill each other on the streets of Verona. Every time a member of one of the two families dies in a fight, his relatives demand the blood of his killer. As a result of the feud, if Romeo is discovered with Juliet by her family, he will be killed. Once Romeo is banished, the only way that Juliet can avoid being married to someone else is to take a potion that apparently killed her, so that she is buried with the bodies of her slain relatives. In this violent, death-filled world, the movement of the story from love at first sight to the union of the lovers in death seems almost inevitable.

'Romeo and Juliet' is considered a love tragedy because Romeo and Juliet both died due to a sequence of dramatic and distressing acts related to their love for each other. The play has elements of comedy which serve to distinguish it from more traditional Greek tragedies. Also, a conventional literary tragedy features a dramatic death of a high-ranking character, not a story's protagonist."[9-10]

While they watched the film, they were gripped with the exciting and fearful moments which put her in a deep emotional mood. The film showed some thrilling scenes of love and romance they had to talk about when they finished. The death of the duo protagonists was indeed a tragedy that deeply touched them.

Barry commented and said, "God forbid that it should happen to a couple in love in real life."

Priscilla corrected him and said, "It's a terrible tragedy, but it's a true life story based on two real lovers who lived in Verona, Italy and they died for each other in 1303."

"Oh my God, I've always thought it was a fiction," said Barry.

When they finished watching the film, they got dressed and went straight to the restaurant to have their meal. They had pizza, vegetables, fruits, and fresh fruit drinks to flush it down. They also had a bottle of wine at the bar. And they left and went back to their suite after relaxing a while.

When they got back to the suite, they sat in front of the television while their instrumental jazz music played in the background. Later on they went out to have a walk around the hotel and the seaside. They saw the beautiful scenes and decorations around the hotel and the seaside which was pretty cool with a cool breeze blowing. They held hands together as they walked on the street chatting and laughing, but they could not stay outside for long because of the cold as it started getting nippy.

They got back to their suite and sat on the sofa in front of their television having conversation about the things they would do in the future as husband and wife while their music also played.

And he asked her, "Would you like us to move out of Edinburgh in the future?"

Priscilla answered and said, "Why?"

"That's question for question. I need an answer," Barry said.

"Sorry, yes I would like us to move to somewhere else in the future because at some point Edinburgh may become boring," said Priscilla. She continued and said, "We can have a change of environment. Can we move down to Florida in the United States of America?"

Barry replied, "Florida will be great for holiday, but I'm talking about a place to live in. I am thinking of London as a place we can move to in the future. I like it because it's the capital city of Britain and also a commercial city. As a banker based in Edinburgh, I noticed that most of our business deals are connected with our London branch."

"Honey, you are the head, whatever decision you make, I am ready to follow and support you," said Priscilla. While they sat talking, they started feeling sleepy and they decided to get together to pray and went to bed afterwards and slept.

Chapter Six: Day 6 – Friday

Setting goals in marriage and life

They woke up and straightaway commenced their morning devotion, singing praise to God, and praying. After that, they decided to work on setting goals for their marriage. They started to set different short-term and long-term goals to help their marriage. The goals they set are subject to review from time to time. Priscilla asked Barry,

"WHAT ARE GOALS, AND HOW DO WE SET AND ACHIEVE THEM?"

Barry answered saying, *Habakkuk 2:2-3,*

> *2And the Lord answered me, and said, write the vision, and make it plain upon tables, that he may run that readeth it.*

> *3For the vision is yet for an appointed time, but at the end it shall speak, and not lie: though it tarry, wait for it; because it will surely come, it will not tarry.*

From this scripture, you can see that it's important for us to write our visions, dreams, or goals down. When you write it down, it's no longer guesswork, but it becomes concrete. The essence of setting goals is to give direction and guidance in order to achieve desired targets. Goals stop us from living life aimlessly.

A goal or a vision is simply a blueprint, clearly set out in writing to be achieved for a specific period. What a satellite navigation system is to a car driver is what your goal is to you. It helps guide you to get to your desired destination. When you set out to build a house, you draw a plan. Similarly, you also have to carefully design your life and set out to live out your dreams by putting one block upon another until your life appears as you have planned it to be. We can truly be the architect of our own life today by clearly writing our goals and working towards achieving them.

To live your life without goals, is to live life without direction, or aimlessly. It's like playing football without goalposts. Therefore, with no target to aim at, no goal will be scored. This sort of life is clearly a life of defeat, and failure. It's important to note the following when we set goals.

THINGS TO NOTE ABOUT GOALS

1. Your goal must be specific.
2. You have to write your goal in a present continuous way. For example, I am losing weight. You can also write it in an affirmative way.
3. Your goal must be measurable in order to monitor progress. For example, my target is to lose weight from 100kg down to 80kg.
4. Your goal must be time-bound or have a deadline. The weight loss goal should therefore be written as – My target is to lose weight from 100kg down to 80kg by the 31st December next year.

5. You must work on your goals daily, like a ritual. Continue to do little things daily that will help you achieve your goals. Your brain responds to your goals as you work on it daily.

6. Your goals must be clear and precise.

7. You must have strategies, tactics, and a workable process for your goals. Therefore, develop a plan of action to follow through in order to achieve your desired goals.

8. You must be committed to your goals.

9. You must break off from habits that act as a barrier to achieving your goals, and develop the right new habits, beliefs, and values that will enable you achieve your goals.

10. You must continually focus on positive things that will help you achieve your desired goals.

11. You must surround yourself with the right positive people who will support your goals rather than negative people who will tell you your goals are not achievable to discourage you.

12. Meditate, affirm, declare, and visualise your goals daily.

13. You must get rid of all fears, doubts, and unworthiness regarding your goals.[11]

We will now go ahead to set some goals for our marriage, and we will set the following goals:

SPIRITUAL AND PERSONAL DEVELOPMENT GOALS

This is the most important goal for the couple because the spiritual rules the physical. They agreed that they will do Bible Study together at least four times a week for a minimum of an hour each session, and they will both minister to each other, sharing the Word of God.

They also agreed that they will pray, and sing praises unto the Lord daily. They have to attend a church service every Sunday and at least one more service during the week to help them connect to church corporate anointing to build themselves up. They also agreed that they will become workers in the church. Barry says he will join the church finance team, while Priscilla decides to join the children's department as a teacher and helper.

Apart from doing Bible study together, they also decided that they will read one Christian book or any other book of interest they chose every month and discuss it together. This will help keep them alert mentally.

Finally, as part of their spiritual exercise and goal, they agreed they will fast at least once every week preferably on Sundays. This can be reviewed and possibly be increased if there is a challenge they need to deal with. They also agreed to participate in every corporate fasting declared by the church. Fasting is important for Christians. Scriptural references on fasting include Matthew 6:17-18, and Isaiah 58:6.

FAMILY GOALS

They agreed together that they would like to have a maximum of three children, irrespective of the sex of the children. And Priscilla said she would prefer to have all three children with a maximum of a two years gap in between. This means that they should be done with having children within five years, and proper family planning is needed to ensure that after the third baby some sort of contraceptives will now be used to stop unwanted pregnancies, like the use of a coil or injections by her or condoms by him. Barry said he is very happy with the proposal, and they will both work towards that.

And she asked him, "How often do we need to have sex weekly?"

They started laughing as Barry answered and said, "Sex is absolutely going to be daily and unlimited."

And she laughed and said, "I hear you. Mind you we didn't have sex yesterday, and I'm glad we didn't as it helps to recuperate, and we will not have sex again today please. I need to rest."

Barry said, "We can have sex about four to five days weekly."

"That's fine," agreed Priscilla. She continued, saying, "Let's pray for the strength to accomplish that. We are young and active now. Hopefully it will continue to be so when we are old." And they started laughing.

Priscilla added again, "This also means we have to be true and honest to each other, not making flimsy excuses not to make love, as well as not committing adultery."

When she said that, Barry's conscience pricked him as he remembered Anna Murray, his former mistress, and he said, "I agree with you darling."

HEALTH GOALS

They agreed to work out together in the gym at least twice every week for a minimum of one hour per session. They agreed that they will also cut down on carbohydrates, sugar, and fatty food and concentrate more on fruit, vegetables, and proteins. They decide not to take any alcohol and also avoid smoking completely. At the moment, Barry weighs 80 kg and Priscilla weighs 70 kg, and they intend to keep it like that for the next five years at least and possibly longer than that. They have both been below that weight for a decade since they first met and started courting. So it's possible to keep maintaining it for much longer.

Part of their health goals also means having regular medical checkups involving blood test, or urinary test, to reveal the state of the body organs, and any disease, dental care, eye test, prostate cancer test, breast cancer tests and so on.

They also agree that they will try and resolve any issues amicably without raising their voices, and not involve third parties, as that can escalate matters, and they will have respect for one another especially with their mode of communication. All these will help keep the marriage healthy.

FINANCIAL GOALS

Barry is a Bank Manager with the National Bank Limited, Edinburgh Branch, earning a very fat salary, and other benefits. Priscilla is a Mathematics teacher in a secondary school also in Edinburgh.

They both agreed that they will depend on God to run their finances. Therefore, they agreed that they will always honour God with their 10% tithes on their gross income plus offerings. They know what the Bible says, and have decided to practice consistently the following scriptures on tithing - Malachi 3:10, Proverbs 3:9-10, Leviticus 27:30-32, and Hebrews 7:1-10. They believe that as they honour God with their tithes faithfully, God will help them supernaturally and they will receive the blessings the Lord promised He will release to givers.

They plan to have a mortgage together as soon as they get back to Edinburgh, and they will also have to open a joint account, making savings towards any emergency and their future.

In the meantime, they intend to commence investments in shares and bonds and Barry, being a banker, will handle that.

They also discussed the possibility of setting up a business in future. They agreed that further discussions will be made concerning that in future.

To help support the family finance, Priscilla decided to start giving classes as a personal tutor for children whose parents are willing to hire her to teach Mathematics.

They spent a good part of their morning discussing and planning for the future, and they wrote everything down to make it concrete. When they finished writing their goals, they had their bath and proceeded to the restaurant to eat.

They had their delicious breakfast and went back to their suite where they continued to talk about their future plans together. And Priscilla said, "Honey, I would like a change of career at some stage in the future, from being a teacher to the entertainment industry. To be more specific, I like theatre and drama."

"How are you going to do that?" Barry asked. He continued and said, "You should have studied that at university instead of Mathematics."

Priscilla said, "I have a flare for it, and I don't have to study it at university before I can do it anyway. I can take some training and also learn while on the job."

Barry said, "That's great. I'm ready to support you darling to realise your dreams as a film superstar."

"Thanks darling," said Priscilla.

"Let's watch the film - *Indecent Proposal*," says Priscilla.

Barry replied, "Yeah. That's fine by me. I've been looking forward to seeing that film."

She went ahead and pulled the film from the internet and also got out a bottle of *Chateau de Fleur* non-alcoholic sparkling wine with two glasses and served for the two of them while they said, "Cheers!" and settled down to watch this breathtaking film.

Priscilla said, "This exciting 1993 American drama is based on the novel of the same name by Jack Engelhard. It was directed by Adrian Lyne and stars Robert Redford, Demi Moore, and Woody Harrelson. David (Woody Harrelson) and Diana Murphy (Demi Moore) are a couple in love with a bright future. David is an architect while Diana is a real estate agent. They have been together since high school and got married. Everything goes well until the recession strikes and they go through financial turmoil. In their last attempt to revive their financial situation they decide to gamble in Vegas where they met John Cage (Robert Redwood), a billionaire, who offered them a million dollars to spend the night with Diana. Out of desperation, they agree to do it and forget it forever. Unfortunately, this became a crack in their marriage which widened and eventually tore them apart as it begins to erode their relationship and Diana started falling for John. Will David be able to win her back?

The moral of this film – No matter how poverty-stricken a couple may be, they should be contented with whatever they have and believe in God to make things better for them rather than take the risk of the wife spending one night with a billionaire for a million dollars or whatever amount whatsoever. This is not biblical, it's devastating, and can effectively end a marriage. This is a must-watch film for a greedy couple. From this film, it seems money can buy love and some feeble-minded people. But as a Christian, one must be firm and adhere to biblical standards in their marriage."[12-13]

After giving a narration of the film, Barry said, "Thank you very much darling." He asked Priscilla, "Do you have any scripture to admonish this Indecent Proposal couple?"

"Yes, I do," said Priscilla, "Their main problem is that they lacked contentment, and discipline. The Bible says we have to learn to be contented and that's exactly what they need to do. *Philippians 4:11-12* says,

[11]Not that I speak in respect of want: for I have learned, in whatsoever state I am, therewith to be content.

[12]I know both how to be abased, and I know how to abound: every where and in all things I am instructed both to be full and to be hungry, both to abound and to suffer need."

When they finished seeing the film, they went down to the restaurant to have their rice menu lunch which was very delicious. While they had lunch they talked about the indecent proposal film. And Barry asked her, "Would you sleep with another man for one night for a million dollars darling?"

She replied, "God forbid! And I forbid! Not even for all the money in this world. I will not sleep with another man. I have the fear of God."

And that answer strengthened him as he said, "Great! You are a wise woman. I love you honey." And he drew near to her and kissed her.

They went back to their suite to continue relaxing and listening to love songs. While they were seated on the sofa, she rested her body on him while he gently caressed her. And she said, "Honey, please keep touching me, I'm enjoying the gentle touch."

He replied, "You will pay a million dollars for the touch."

"I will pay two million dollars instead," she said and giggled.

As he touched her, she fell asleep and they got on the bed and slept till late in the evening. They got up and decided to still go to the restaurant to have a light dinner, and some wine and stay in the bar and relax and see people. When they got to the restaurant, they had a light dinner before going into the bar for drinks where they stayed until late at night. While they were at the bar, they met Pedro, who kept them busy with stories about the Island including some of the landmarks. They later left him and went straight back to their suite to sleep.

Chapter Seven: Day 7 – Saturday

Questions and answers to various marriage issues

They got up early in the morning and sang praises unto God and prayed. When they finished, they settled down for their Bible Study and Priscilla said to Barry, "I have a number of questions to ask you today."

She started by asking:

PRISCILLA: SHOULD A CHRISTIAN PRACTICE ANAL SEX?

BARRY: A Christian should not practice anal sex. I strongly advise against it. I don't do it with you darling because I consider it dirty. *Firstly*, the anus is meant for faeces, and not for penis penetration. *Secondly*, doing that can lead to contracting disease. *Thirdly*, the Bible says in *1 Corinthians 14:40*, *"Let all things be done decently and in order."* Having anal sex is not decent and orderly at all and should therefore not be practiced.

PRISCILLA: Thanks for the answer darling. My second question is,

SHOULD A CHRISTIAN PRACTICE ORAL SEX?

BARRY: Again, this is a question that calls for a grey answer and I would like to sit on the fence here as I say YES and NO. It's a matter of choice to the Christian who decides to do it. To start with, we don't do oral sex, and I personally don't see it as decent. The Bible says in **1 Corinthians 14:40**, *"Let all things be done decently and in order."* God created the penis to go into the vagina, and food for the mouth. Why should there be a swapping around? Why should the penis be put into the mouth? It's awkward. The female sex organ vagina is very much open and exposed, and my advice to any man who wants to practice oral sex with a woman is that they should ensure the vagina is thoroughly washed to avoid a bad smell and contracting a disease. The pubic hair should be cut short. Oral sex is one way of getting a woman to reach orgasm provided it is done gently because the vagina is a soft delicate part of the body. The man should kiss, and suck the clitoris gently and the inner parts of the vagina to turn the woman on and make her wet. Afterwards, the man should thoroughly clean his mouth with mouthwash. Besides, oral sex should not replace actual sex.

On the other hand, the woman can also engage in oral sex with the man. Again, the penis must be thoroughly washed to avoid a bad smell and contracting a disease. The pubic hair needs to be short. The penis is a soft and tender male organ, and therefore should be handled with care and gently as it is caressed, kissed, and sucked to arouse the man. The man must not ejaculate into the woman's mouth. He has to control that. The woman should not bite the penis, and she should wash her mouth with mouthwash thoroughly after this exercise.

It is important to also mention here that oral sex should be with consent and not something that you will compel your partner to do, or get upset about if he or she is not willing to do it. Both parties have to do it with a consensus and enjoy it together.

PRISCILLA: Well answered darling. My next question is,

SHOULD A COUPLE HAVE SEX DURING THE WOMAN'S MENSTRUAL PERIOD?

BARRY: Again, I don't have sex with you during your menstrual period because I see it as dirty being a discharge from the body, and it's biblically wrong to do so. The Bible says in **Leviticus 15:19**, "*And if a woman have an issue, and her issue in her flesh be blood, she shall be put apart seven days: and whosoever toucheth her shall be unclean until the even.*"

However, if a couple must really have sex during her mensuration, she must wash her vagina thoroughly to get rid of the blood, and the man should use condoms for protection so as not to contract an infection or disease. For hygiene purposes, it is better to avoid sex during this period.

PRISCILLA: Thanks for your answer honey. My next question is,

SHOULD A COUPLE BE WITHOUT SEX DURING PREGNANCY?"

BARRY: A couple can still continue to have sex throughout a woman's pregnançy, according to the information I gathered from experienced married people, medical research, and books I read. The only thing that needs to be done is that the couple must choose very convenient positions, and the man must ensure he is gentle with his penis during sex.

PRISCILLA: Thanks a lot for your answer. My next question is,

SHOULD A CHRISTIAN INDULGE IN BREAST ENLARGEMENT, BUTTOCKS ADJUSTMENT OR TRANSGENDER ACTIONS?

BARRY: The Bible says in *Psalm 139:14*, "*I will praise thee; for I am fearfully and wonderfully made: marvellous are thy works; and that my soul knoweth right well.*" Based on what this scripture says, I would not support a Christian trying to recreate themself into something else because they want to look good. That's an insult to the wisdom of God. He has created you the way He feels you should be. So be proud of yourself and believe in yourself. Have self-esteem and be proud of yourself. Never look down on yourself or shape. See yourself as the best. If however, a person is seeking changes to any part of the body based on serious medical grounds, that's understandable, but not because of beauty and fashion. Note that some people have got serious health problems, and some others died as a result of complications arising from breast enlargement, buttocks adjustments, and sex changes. These things may not make you look sexy as some people are deceived to believe. Therefore, it's important not to tamper with your beautiful body which is also the temple of the Holy Spirit. Defile it, and God will destroy you. – See *1 Corinthians 3:17*.

PRISCILLA: Thank you very much for your answer. My next question is,

SHOULD A CHRISTIAN HAVE TATTOOS AND INDULGE IN TRANSVESTITE ACTIONS?

BARRY: I will try to give you a satisfactory answer based on what the scriptures say. I would like to bring up *1 Corinthians 14:40* again. It says, *"Let all things be done decently and in order."* The Bible states in *Leviticus 19:28 of The Living Bible*, *"You shall not cut yourselves nor put tattoo marks upon yourselves in connection with funeral rites; I am the Lord."* The Bible also says in *Deuteronomy 22:5*, *"The woman shall not wear that which pertaineth unto a man, neither shall a man put on a woman's garment: for all that do so are abomination unto the LORD thy God."*

As we have seen from the above scriptures, the Bible does not approve of a Christian wearing tattoos or dressing and acting like the opposite sex. It is not decent, and it's also an abomination. The danger with such acts is that when people start, they hardly stop. For example, I have seen some people start with a tiny tattoo and eventually get obsessed about tattoos and end up having it all over their body, making them look horrible and unfortunately, it is not reversible. Therefore, my advice is, don't even start. You don't even need to have any tattoos on your body because you are fearfully and wonderfully made by God already. While we are on this topic, I would like to briefly mention about the idea of men piercing their ears and nose, and wearing earrings and nose ring. This is also a grey area but I think wearing earrings and nose ring should be left to women. It's not decent for a man. You are handsome! You are beautiful! Avoid inferiority complex. Be natural and be yourself. These things will not make you look sexier as some people are deceived to believe.

The Bible says in 1 Corinthians 6:19 that our body is the temple of the Holy Spirit. And 1 Corinthians 3:16-17 further states that anyone who defiles this temple, God will destroy him. Why defile your body with tattoos? It is important to also note that to have tattoos all over your body and face could hinder your chances of getting a good job, and a partner to marry. This answer is not meant to judge anyone. It is simply a correction in line with biblical principles. It's good for a Christian to have a godly outlook.

Finally, the Bible says in **Romans 12:1**, *"I beseech you therefore, brethren, by the mercies of God, that ye present your bodies a living sacrifice, holy, acceptable unto God, which is your reasonable service."*

PRISCILLA: Thanks for your answer darling. My next question is,

SHOULD A CHRISTIAN BE A HOMOSEXUAL OR LESBIAN?

BARRY: The Bible is against homosexual activity, and it should therefore not be practiced by a Christian.

Homosexual or gay is the coming together of two men and carrying out sex acts through the anus, which I have said earlier, is dirty and can lead to contraction of diseases. The anus is meant for faeces to exit. It's better to use it to perform the function God designed it for. Let's see what the Bible says in

> *Leviticus 18:22, "Thou shalt not lie with mankind, as with womankind: it is abomination."*

> *Leviticus 20:13, "If a man also lie with mankind, as he lieth with a woman, both of them have committed an abomination: they shall surely be put to death; their blood shall be upon them."*

Similarly, the coming together of two Christian women to perform sex acts as lesbians is not right. God created us to be heterosexuals.

Finally, it's important to note that there is no scripture that supports Lesbian, Gay, Bisexual, and Transgender (LGBT) lifestyles. Therefore, Christians should not practice it. God is against it.

PRISCILLA: Thank you very much, sweetheart, for your brilliant answers. I have really engaged you with questions this morning. However, I have six more questions.

WHAT'S YOUR VIEW ON SAME-SEX MARRIAGE AS A CHRISTIAN?

You can see that some parts of the world are already approving it.

BARRY: I'm not going to beat about the bush here at all. I will simply hit the nail on the head and tell you outright that it is both morally and biblically wrong for a Christian to practice same-sex marriage. From the beginning in the book of Genesis 1:27 and 5:2, the Most High God in His wisdom created male and female, Adam and Eve to be in marriage union. He did not unite Adam and Adam, or Eve and Eve together. I believe the enemy is seriously polluting the hearts of men and deceiving them to go into same-sex marriage. How will there be procreation with same-sex marriage? What is the rationale behind such an ungodly act? We have already seen from your last question that the Bible is against gay and lesbian lifestyle, and in the same vein, same-sex marriage is hereby utterly condemned.

PRISCILLA: Thanks for your brilliant answer. I am learning new things today and I'm so excited about it darling. Thank God for this wonderful opportunity for us to get together and engage in Bible study. My next question is this:

SHOULD A MARRIED CHRISTIAN COUPLE DELIBRATELY DENY ONE ANOTHER SEX AS PUNISHMENT FOR THE WRONG THEY DID?

BARRY: Never! And I repeat, never! That's not romantic, loving, or biblical. The Bible says in *1 Corinthians 7:3-5,*

> *³Let the husband render unto the wife due benevolence: and likewise also the wife unto the husband.*

⁴The wife hath not power of her own body, but the husband: and likewise also the husband hath not power of his own body, but the wife.

⁵Defraud ye not one the other, except it be with consent for a time, that ye may give yourselves to fasting and prayer; and come together again, that Satan tempt you not for your incontinency.

To deny your wife or husband sex as a punishment because of what they did wrong is simply callous, and must not be allowed at all in a marriage. According to the above scriptures, the only period a couple should abstain from sex is a period of spiritual exercise, and that has to be agreed by both parties. The Bible says in **Ephesians 4: 27**, *"Neither give place to the devil."* Once you start denying one another sex, that is tantamount to cracks and opening the door to allowing the enemy, the devil, to come into the marriage, and before you know it, it becomes a stronghold in the sense that the couple gets used to not having sex anymore and that can effectively be the beginning of emotional separation and it is dangerous. Constant romance, love, and sex are absolutely necessary for a healthy marriage. And I can even sum it up like this: No sex, no marriage. Marriage without sex is as good as dead.

These days, all sorts of things happen in marriages. One of such things I have heard about and also seen is the case of married couples sleeping in different bedrooms. This is a way of giving place to the devil. You are not co-tenants. Therefore, sleep in the same room and on the same bed with both partners feeling each other's warmth, and caressing each other, and making love regularly as much as possible. Sex refreshes the soul. Enjoy it. Stop making flimsy excuses not to have sex. Avoid excuses like I am tired, I am under menstruation when you are not, I will be late to work and I need to be early, I asked you for money, this and that and you have not done it. These are all nonsense excuses. I have seen young couples who have been without sex for six months, one year, and even over two years. This shouldn't be. Don't give place to the devil. Take advantage of what you are reading right now in this book and have sex with your partner today, and you will truly be glad you did as it will help restore your marriage.

PRISCILLA: Thank you very much for your beautiful answer darling, and I admire your courage to tell the truth in line with the scriptures. My next question is this:

WHAT IS YOUR OPINION ABOUT DIVORCE AFTER MARRIAGE?

BARRY: I would like to first say that God hates divorce, and the Bible states that in **Malachi 2:16** *saying, "For the* LORD, *the God of Israel, saith that he hateth putting away: for one covereth violence with his garment, saith the* LORD *of hosts: therefore take heed to your spirit, that ye deal not treacherously."* Jesus also spoke strongly against divorce in **Matthew 19:1-9** and in verse 9, He specifically said, *"And I say unto you, Whosoever shall put away his wife, except it be for fornication, and shall marry another, committeth adultery: and whoso marrieth her which is put away doth commit adultery."* From this scripture, it means that the only ground a married

Christian couple could divorce is fornication which is also forgivable anyway.

However, the courts also grant Christians divorce based on the grounds of *'unreasonable behaviour,'* and this covers a whole lot of issues including violence, deceit, sexual denial, financial abuse, etc. Marriage is meant to be a lifetime covenant as Jesus pointed out in **Matthew 19:6** saying, *"Wherefore they are no more twain, but one flesh. What therefore God hath joined together, let not man put asunder."* No man or court is supposed to put asunder any marriage, but the wickedness of some people has led to that. That's why Moses also approved divorce according to verses 7–8. The Bible says in *1 Timothy 1:8*, *"But we know that the law is good, if a man use it lawfully;"* Use the law to correct any case of injustice.

Firstly, my personal opinion is going to be along the line of unreasonable behaviour in marriage, and it should be a decision that should be taken solely by the married person involved, and through the leading of the Holy Spirit and the wisdom of God. My personal opinion is that you should *consider* getting a divorce if you have been fraudulently deceived into a marriage. For example, a man is impotent and hides it from you and marries you as a woman, and you discover after marriage that he cannot perform his sexual obligations as a man. No erection! *Consider* a divorce. That's fraud and deceit. Again, if, for example, a woman has no womb because it has been taken out for any reason whatsoever, or has stopped menstruating and therefore cannot be pregnant, and did not disclose it and got married to you. And this means she can't be pregnant. That's fraud and deceit. *Consider* a divorce.

Secondly, if before marriage your partner did not disclose some serious disease such as HIV AIDS, and you later find out after marriage, you need to *consider* a divorce because when you contract such disease through sex, it will kill you.

Thirdly, you must not allow your partner out of envy and wickedness to fight and stop your God given vision or dream. *Consider* a divorce if this happens because marriage should not stop you from fulfilling God's purpose or assignment for you on earth.

Finally, if you are in an abusive relationship whether verbal or physical with actual bodily harm, emotional torment, or threats of death, you may also have to *consider* a divorce once there is substantial evidence to back this up. The reason why I have to mention this is because I have seen and heard of several cases where a husband killed a wife or a wife killed a husband in an abusive relationship. Why do you have to die because of marriage? And what's the point of living with an enemy who wants to kill you? *I repeat again, this decision should only be taken solely by the married person involved, and through the leading of the Holy Spirit and the wisdom of God.*

PRISCILLA: Thank you very much for your brilliant answer darling, and I admire your courage to tell the truth in line with the scriptures. My next question is,

SHOULD A CHRISTIAN COUPLE FACING SERIOUS QUARRELS IN MARRIAGE SEPARATE?

BARRY: There is no place in the Bible where it is written expressly that a couple can separate for whatsoever reason.

Therefore, my answer is NO. A couple should not separate at all. There should not be discontinuity in marriage even if it is temporary. The Bible says in *Ephesians 4:27*, *"Neither give place to the devil."* The danger of separation is that it might well be an open door for the devil to come into the marriage and do a lot more damage than good. For example, it can be an opportunity for any of the couple to start having sexual affairs with another person. Therefore, effectively close the door against separation. How? *Ephesians 4:26, "Be ye angry, and sin not: let not the sun go down upon your wrath:"* Resolve all quarrels same day before you sleep and avoid getting a third party involved. Use the Word of God as your final umpire to resolve disagreements. The Bible covers all areas of life. Invite the Holy Spirit to minister to you as a couple. Seek the counsel of wise, Holy Spirit-filled men, only after you have committed the matter to God.

PRISCILLA: Thanks for your brilliant answer darling. My next question is,

WHAT ARE THE MAIN CAUSES OF SEPARTION AND DIVORCE IN MARRIAGE?

BARRY: Separation and divorce in marriage are caused by a lot of things, but I will just mention a few things in my opinion that cause it.

Firstly, marrying the wrong person who is not the bone of your bone and the flesh of your flesh can easily lead to separation and divorce. Therefore, it's important to ask the Holy Spirit to lead and direct you to the person God has ordained for you to marry. Once you get this right, you are not likely to experience separation and divorce. Investigate whoever you want to marry by asking them loads of questions during courtship which will reveal who they are. If they refuse to answer your questions, then they are not open-minded, and therefore have things to hide, don't proceed. Don't be carried away by the fact that they claim to be born again Christian, and also speak in tongues. There are a lot of lies and deceit in relationships nowadays, even among so-called Christians. Once you discover a lie or deceit, seriously consider pulling out of the courtship.

Secondly, lack of knowledge about marriage. Marriage is one of the institutions people horridly dabble in without adequate knowledge. Here, you find people who don't know what the scriptures says about marriage, people who have never read a single book on marriage, never listened to a preaching or message on marriage, never been to a marriage seminar, workshop, or counseling session getting married. What will such a person do when they get into marriage? They will wreck the marriage because of a lack of knowledge. Hosea 4:6 says my people are destroyed for lack of knowledge. Ensure you and your partner get proper training before you marry.

Thirdly, lack of commitment to marriage vows can also lead to separation and divorce. These days, people marry and fail to commit, invest, and sacrifice anything into their marriage. They break marriage vows with impunity and without remorse or repentance. Shame! A lot of people get married for the wrong reason – What can I get out of this marriage? They are simply gold diggers. They are not prepared to do anything to enhance the value of their partner. They only want to receive and give nothing in the marriage. Selfish! Hey! Marriage should be a mutual relationship. The same goes for other kinds of relationship like business relationships. Be committed to your partner. That's true relationship.

Fourthly, lack of respect for your partner can also lead to separation and divorce. The simple rule here is, don't do what the Bible is against or what your partner doesn't like. And don't respect other people more than your partner. Hold your partner in high esteem. Praise him, regard him, and love him wholeheartedly.

Fifthly, unfaithfulness can also lead to separation and divorce. Avoid cheating on your partner. It's derogatory, tormenting, and a sin to do so. It's called adultery. Once you are married, you must strictly stick to your partner for your sexual satisfaction. No extramarital affairs are allowed because it can lead to separation and divorce. That's it for now.

PRISCILLA: Thanks a lot for your lovely answer. My last question is,

SHOULD A CHRISTIAN MASTURBATE?

BARRY: This is another grey area because I don't have a scripture to back my answer up. However, making reference to *1 Corinthians 14:40* again, that says *"Let all things be done decently and in order,"* I will prefer to allow the Holy Spirit to minister to every reader personally based on this scripture the truth about masturbation. My only advice is that if anyone cannot bear to be alone as a Christian, they should simply marry rather than burn with passion. Unfortunately, some married people who their partners don't satisfy sexually also masturbate. Therefore, it's better to discipline your flesh as a Christian. Also avoid pornographic materials.

When Barry finished his ministration, she stood up and started clapping saying, "Thank you very much honey, for your wonderful teaching today. You have cleared the air regarding some grey areas and I'm so pleased you did it skillfully, backing your answers with appropriate scriptures."

"You are welcome sweetheart," Barry replied. "The truth is bitter, but it must be said. For everything I have said today, I had to use a biblical approach and standard to resolve it."

Priscilla said, "I agree with you honey."

They started undressing getting ready for a bath, and as they saw each other's nakedness, Barry got a full erection and he held her and said, "You are very beautiful, and I love you."

She bowed her head down a little with a charming smile and said, "I love you too darling."

They have not had sex for the past two days so they are now refreshed and virile ready to have intense sex. He grabbed her moderate breasts and began to fondle and suck them while fingering her as she lay on the bed with her eyes closed and absolutely in a relaxed mood as he also massaged her. This went on for a long while to turn her on very well and they got intoxicated with love and he went into her and had carnal knowledge of her. And as the sex session became intense, she made very romantic utterances saying, "Honey, I love you very much. I want more of it. More! Yeah, I say more! Harder!"

Barry intensified his swinging motion faster and harder and eventually he ejaculated and they end the sex session while he continued to cuddle and kiss her as she rested her body on him. After a while, they got into the bathroom and had a good bath, dressed up and went down to the hotel restaurant to have their breakfast.

They served their usual English breakfast with assorted items, collected a variety of drinks to go with it and went and sat down at a table for two and began to eat. Barry took some sausage and fed her, and she said, "Thanks darling."

Whilst they ate, Barry said, "It's good to be on honeymoon. I feel like I'm just with you alone in this whole world like Adam and Eve in a paradise."

She laughed and asked, "Why did you say that?"

Barry replied, "That's because we have hardly communicated with people on the phone since we arrived in Majorca. We hardly touch our phones."

"That's true," said Priscilla. She continued saying, "That reminds me, as we get back to the suite, I'm going to call my Dad and Mary, my cousin, to say hello."

After the sumptuous meal, they made their way back to their suite holding hands and chatting, and giggling.

As they got back to the suite, she got her phone out and turned it on and discovered she had a lot of messages and missed calls. She rang her father and as she got through she said, "Hello Dad, this is Mrs Evans on the line. How are you, mum and the rest of the family?"

With a heart full of joy and smiles he said, "We are fine Mrs Evans. I like your new name."

They started laughing. And he said, "It's good to hear from you darling. How is your husband?"

"He is very fine taking very good care of me," Priscilla replied.

Her father continued, "It's good to hear that. You only have one more week left for your honeymoon in Majorca."

She exclaimed saying, "Please don't remind me of that Dad! I wish this honeymoon could last forever. Anyway, I've got to go Dad. Please extend my sincere regards to everyone."

They both said, "Bye," and ended the call.

She scrolled down her phone address book and located Mary Jenkins, her cousin's number and called her. As she got through, they both screamed excitedly as Priscilla says, "How are you doing Hotdog?"

Mary replied and said, "I'm fine Priscooh! It's great to hear from you. How is your husband?"

"All is indeed well," Priscilla answered. She continued and said, "Barry is fine. He is the best husband in the world, and I pray this romance will last forever."

Mary said, "Oh! It's good to know all is well indeed."

They carried on their conversation for a little while about the good times they were having on the island of Majorca and ended the call. Meanwhile, Barry was also busy checking his phone messages, and returning some important calls to his family and friends.

They got out all their dirty laundry and sent it off for cleaning. They got ready and went down to the special unisex salon there at the Champion 5-star hotel to have their hair done, and a manicure and a pedicure. It's a well-organised salon with modern equipment, experienced staff, and the proprietor, a young Spanish girl called Catalina is very friendly. They were warmly welcomed to the Salon and had their hair nicely done, plus a manicure and a pedicure. While they were there, the television was on and instrumental jazz music played in the background at a mid-tempo level. They were also given sweets, soft drinks, and water. Good service! When they finished, they went back to their suite. "Tomorrow is New Year, and Sunday, and we will be at the Cathedral de Mallorca for 9 am service," says Barry.

She replied and said, "I'm looking forward to be there tomorrow."

And he replied and said, "Me too."

They sat next to each other on the sofa watching television. Barry said, "Please change the channel darling to a sports channel. Let's see the *Barcelona versus Real Madrid* game."

She changed the channel and the match has already started. Just five minutes into the match. They both like football. And they are happy to see the following stars – Christiano Ronaldo, Gareth Bale, Sergio Ramos, Marco Asensio, and Marcelo Viera on the pitch playing for Real Madrid. Barcelona's lineup also includes the following top players – Lionel Messi, Luis Suarez, Gerald Pique, Paulinho, and Andres Iniesta. After seeing the lineup of the two sides, they shouted and said, "This game is going to be interesting and tough." The stadium was packed full and there were roaring shouts of approval, while the commentator was heard in the background delivering the commentary in Spanish. She got up and got out a bottle of *Senorio de la Tautila Espumoso Rosado* non-alcoholic Spanish wine and two glasses and served. And they lifted up their glasses and said, "Cheers!"

Barry sipped a little and said, "This wine is nice. Thanks darling."

"You are welcome," replied Priscilla.

They are both fans of Real Madrid. It had to be so after she had seen families turn apart just because they were fans of different clubs. Priscilla thought to herself as a wise submissive wife ready to let her husband lead and for her to follow, who also desires peace and has resolved that football will not bring unnecessary arguments in their marriage. Regarding football and most things, her policy is that whatever my husband likes is what I like. She was immediately quickened to remember *Genesis 2:18*, *"And the* LORD *God said, It is not good that the man should be alone; I will make him an help meet for him."*

A wife is a help meet to support a husband in his vision. That's why the husband marries the wife and pays the bride price, and she changes her maiden name from Priscilla Jenkins to Priscilla Evans. The husband is to lead, and every wise woman who truly desires to build her home follows the husband as the help meet God has created her to be, by supporting the husband's vision. The Bible also says in *1 Corinthians 11:3* that the husband is the head of the wife. And *Proverbs 14:1* says, *"Every wise woman buildeth her house: but the foolish plucketh it down with her hands."*

She is determined to do all she can humanly do to build her home. She has a vision to follow the footsteps of the *Proverbs 31:10-31* wife and excel in all things. That's her dream for her marriage and family.

The game carried on with both sides making a positive impact every now and then with impressive strikes. Ronaldo, being a highly talented and skilled player made wonderful moves, motivating his teammates. Towards the end of the first half, Real Madrid mounted more and more pressure on Barcelona and in a twinkle of an eye there was a little defensive error and Ronaldo capitalised on it and meandered through, dribbling the defender and stylishly deceived the goalkeeper and netted the ball and the whole stadium went up in a big cheer and roar of shouts with people clapping, singing, and dancing. The Commentator is also there skillfully delivering the commentary. The scores immediately appeared on the scoreboard.

As Barry began to shout, clap, and dance for the one-goal lead by Real Madrid, his wife wisely joined the husband to celebrate the goal. That's the right spirit of followership and unity she learnt during the marriage counseling sessions before their wedding and also in line with the Word of God. Barry held his wife in excitement and said, "I love you darling. We are winning the game."

And she replied and said, "I love you too honey. We are winning indeed." As she said that she put up a cheerful smile. Barry held her close to himself and kissed her while they close their eyes and as they disengaged from the kissing, she said, "I love you." And he replied, "I love you too. You are sweeter than honey."

The second half of the game resumed after a fifteen-minute break, which also gave them a break to kiss and caress one another romantically. As the second half resumed and continued, there came an opening and

Lionel Messi blasted an unexpected shot from midfield with his left foot and netted a goal, surprising everybody and equalising the game. That saddened Barry, and she also joined the husband to feel bad about the goal. There was also a great cheer and roaring of singing from Barcelona fans when the goal was scored.

As the game continued, there came another opening and Gareth Bale in partnership with Ronaldo made wonderful passes which tore apart Barcelona's defence and Gareth scored and there came forth shouts of joy in the crowded stadium. The game is played in Madrid, so Real Madrid also had a home advantage. Eventually, the game ended as 2–1 victory for Real and Barry celebrated with his wife by topping up more wine as they laughed and discussed the game together after the wonderful match. They dressed up and went down to the restaurant to eat.

They got there and were served delicious rice, fish, stew, vegetables, fruits, pudding, and drinks to flush down the food. They sat down to eat the sumptuous meal and she took some fish and fed her husband and he said, "Thank you darling. This fish is sweet."

He also took some of the rice and fed her, and she said, "Thank you honey. The rice tastes nice."

They carried on eating and as they ate, they discussed the football. Real Madrid is on the top of the league table with the win and Barcelona is in the third position. Barry went ahead and highlighted two scenes he loved about the football match and his wife affirmed and approved of the two scenes. They are both happy and satisfied with the meal and relaxed for a while before they went back to their suite.

When they got back to their suite, they put on their television. And they agreed they will go to bed early to be able to get to church before the 9am official starting time. While they talked, their suite telephone rang and it's a call from the laundry department saying their clothes are ready. And in five minutes someone is already at the door. Barry got up and opened the door and collected the neatly washed and ironed clothes. Barry put the clothes neatly in the wardrobe.

After a while, they decided to do their night prayers. They began by singing praises unto the Lord, and followed it up with prayers. They thanked God for His protection and provisions for the whole year as they have nearly come to the end of the year. Tomorrow is New Year. They got into their bed and chatted for a while, held one another and kissed and slept.

Chapter Eight: Day 8 – Sunday

Levels of faith

They got up early in the morning and wished one another a Happy New Year. They said their prayers.

Barry prayed saying, "Heavenly Father, we thank you very much for making it possible for us to be alive and well to see this New Year. We ask for your continued peace, protection, excellent health, and prosperity in this New Year. You said in Proverbs 4:18 that the path of the just is like the shinning light that shines more and more unto the perfect day. Let our paths shine brighter and brighter in this New Year and forever. Let our path and life shine from one level of glory to a higher level of glory in Jesus' name."

They both say, "Amen!"

They quickly went into the bathroom and had their bath and dressed up. Priscilla put on a long *Dolce & Gabbana* purple gown with a purple hat to match and nice golden necklace with a pendant. Her makeup was a light one since she is going to the house of the Lord. Everything in moderation! He put on his *Ralph Lauren* navy blue suit, *Versace* red tie with blue stripes to stand out, and *Ermenegildo Zegna* black shoes. They both put on their favourite perfumes to smell nice, and just when they finished dressing, their cab arranged by Champion was ready and as they came out of the hotel, behold it was Antonio waiting to take them. They exchanged greetings saying, "Happy New Year," and they got into the car and he drove them straight to the prestigious Cathedral de Mallorca. Antonio promised to be back after the service to take them back to the hotel.

They exchanged greetings with the Ushers at the entrance saying, "Feliz Año Nuevo." Meaning "Happy New Year," and then collected their bulletins and quietly got into the church to sit where the Ushers directed them to sit for the service. The atmosphere on this service day is quite different from what it was when they came on a tour last week Tuesday. The whole church is lively with people and the presence of God filled the auditorium. They came to church with great expectation that they will receive a word in due season, and a miracle.

They sat down and their eyes kept on moving up and down the magnificent edifice with attractive artworks, lighting, and New Year decorations. They got to church at 8.45am so they spent the fifteen minutes before the 9.00am start time saying a short prayer and reading their bulletin which was mostly in Spanish. At exactly 9am, the service commenced as the Ministers of God came in to the altar and Bishop Juan Diego started conducting the service in Spanish.

He says, "Feliz año nuevo a todos. Por favor, gira y intercambia saludos unos con otros." This means, "Happy New Year to you all. Please go round and exchange greetings with one another."

Mr and Mrs Evans went round and exchanged greetings saying, "Feliz Año Nuevo," with broad smiles, laughter, handshakes, and embraces. After that, they all went back to their respective seats. The first and second readings were taken from Matthew 11:28-30 and John 7:37-39 of the New Testament of the Bible and Bishop Juan Diego stood up and preached based on the Bible readings. They served holy communion and collected offerings and then the benediction and the service was brought to an end. Great!

After the service he asked her, "How do you find the service?"

"Great! It makes a huge difference to try something new," she replied. "I'm delighted to be here."

"So I am," said Barry.

They came out of the church and behold, Antonio was already waiting to take them back to the Champion Hotel. They had to quickly take a few pictures with their mobile phones and then got into the car back to the Champion 5 star hotel.

They went straight to the restaurant to have their breakfast. They served their breakfast with drinks and settled down to eat. "Be careful, darling, not to soil your beautiful dress," said Barry.

She said, "Alright sweetheart."

He cut some bacon and fed her and she said, "Thanks sweetheart." They finished eating and relaxed for a little while and went back to their suite.

As they got back to the suite, they undressed and put on something casual, before they got out their mobile phones and made some important calls to friends and family, wishing them Happy New Year. She called her parents and her cousin Mary Jenkins. Barry also called his parents. And when they finished, they sat down in front of the television.

Barry said to her, "It's your turn to share the Word of God today. Can you do that now?"

"Yes, I will," she answered.

They got up and got out their Bibles and she said, "I will be ministering on the topic:

LEVELS OF FAITH

The Bible gives us the meaning of faith in **Hebrews 11:1** saying, "*Now faith is the substance of things hoped for, the evidence of things not seen.*"

From **Romans 12:3** we also know that, "*...God hath dealt to every man the measure of faith.*" As long as you don't use this measure of faith God has given to you, it will remain dormant. The extent to which you use the measure of faith you have also determines your level of faith which will be discussed. The Bible says that faith without works is dead. Therefore, it's important for us to use our faith to the maximum. God is pleased when we use our faith. That's why the Bible says in **Hebrews 11:6** that, "*But without faith it is impossible to please him: for he that cometh to God must believe that he is, and that he is a rewarder of them that diligently seek him.*"

SO GREAT FAITH

Jesus described the Centurion as a person with such a great faith. His servant was sick and he came to Jesus for help and Jesus told him that He will come to his house, but he said to Jesus that he was not worthy, that He should come under his roof, and that He should just speak the word and he will believe. **Matthew 8:10** says,

"When Jesus heard it, he marvelled, and said to them that followed, Verily I say unto you, I have not found so great faith, no, not in Israel." (Underline mine)

GREAT FAITH

Jesus also described the Woman of Canaan as a person with great faith. Her daughter was seriously sick and she came to Jesus for help. And Jesus said it is not good that the bread meant for the children should be given to dogs. And she answered and said, *"Truth, Lord: yet the dogs eat of the crumbs which fall from their master's table."* Jesus answered her in **Matthew 15:28** that says, *"Then Jesus answered and said unto her, O woman, great is thy faith: be it unto thee even as thou wilt. And her daughter was made whole from that very hour."* (Underline mine)

LITTLE FAITH

Peter and the other disciples saw Jesus walking on water and they marveled. And Peter asked if he should come, and Jesus said he should come. Initially, Peter walked on water, as long as he focused on Jesus, but when he saw the boisterous wind, he cried out for help and started sinking. Read what Jesus said to him below:

Matthew 14:31

> [31]*And immediately Jesus stretched forth his hand, and caught him, and said unto him, O thou of little faith, wherefore didst thou doubt?* (Underline mine)

NO FAITH

There are people who don't use the measure of faith God has given them at all in certain circumstances. The scripture below was the response Jesus gave to his disciples when they were facing a raging storm and they were fearful and cried out for His help. As long as you don't use your faith, it will remain dormant. When a man regularly works out in the gym, his muscles will be built up. Similarly, the more you use your faith, the more your faith will be built up. Use your faith regularly, and it will be built up to the highest level of – So great faith!

Mark 4:40

[40]*And he said unto them, Why are ye so fearful? how is it that ye have <u>no faith?</u>* (Underline mine)

YOUR FAITH HAS MADE YOU WHOLE

Reading the story in the two passages below concerning the Woman with the issue of blood, and Blind Bartimaeus, you will see what Jesus said, *"Thy faith hath made thee whole."* This means that their healing and wholesomeness largely depended on them using their faith without which nothing would have happened. They put their faith into action. Similarly, if you don't start using your faith regarding what you want from God, it's likely nothing will happen because as we saw earlier in **Hebrews 11:6**, *"But without faith it is impossible to please him:"*

Mark 5:34,

> ³⁴*And he said unto her, Daughter, <u>thy faith hath made thee whole</u>; go in peace, and be whole of thy plague.* (Underline mine)

Mark 10:52

> ⁵²*And Jesus said unto him, Go thy way; <u>thy faith hath made thee whole</u>. And immediately he received his sight, and followed Jesus in the way.* (Underline mine)

It's important for us to know the different levels of faith so that we can start using our faith properly. Use so great faith in situations like the Centurion and see miracles happen. It's also interesting to note that we don't need big faith to get things done. As a matter of fact, Jesus said all we need is faith as small as a mustard seed in order to move mountains in **Matthew 17:20,**

> ²⁰*And Jesus said unto them, Because of your unbelief: for verily I say unto you, <u>If ye have faith as a grain of mustard seed</u>, ye shall say unto this mountain, Remove hence to yonder place; and it shall remove; and nothing shall be impossible unto you.* (Underline mine)

Also, if we claim to have faith, and we don't have evidence to prove it, such faith is dead. *James 2:17* says, *"Even so faith, if it hath not works, is dead, being alone."*

The reason why I had to talk about the topic, "Levels of faith," is because, as a couple, we need to constantly express optimism and great faith in all we do. This will keep our marriage strong and healthy.

When she finished her ministration, he started clapping for her and said, "You are a great teacher darling. I love your teaching. You have demonstrated great skill in the use of scriptures and clarity in the way you delivered the message. I'm inspired. Well done."

Priscilla said, "Thanks darling, I thought I was nervous and didn't do well."

Barry replied, "You did absolutely well. Fantastic!"

They settled down again with their notebooks to take notes and found on the internet Pastor Joel Osteen's preaching on faith and began to listen to it. And as he preached they were encouraged more. After that they also listened to Pastor Joyce Meyer's preaching on faith. She made reference to some of the scriptures Priscilla had just used in her teaching regarding levels of faith and Barry said, "Can you see she is making reference to some of the scriptures you just used honey? This shows you are on track."

After she finished her ministration, they decided to also listen to Bishop John Barnes preaching about faith on the internet. And as he ministered, they listened with rapt attention and they could feel the anointing filing up the suite as he ministered. The Word of God came forth with great power and they were deeply touched.

After his ministration, Barry said, "That's it. Let's call it a day with the internet ministrations. What a great way of spending time together on a Sunday and the first day of the new year."

"It's a fruitful day. I enjoyed the teachings," agreed Priscilla.

They got dressed and went down to the restaurant to have their meal. When they finished, they relaxed a bit and decided to go for a walk and as they did that, they held hands chatting and laughing together. The chilly breeze blew them and after a short distance they decided to start making their way back to their suite.

When they came back, they sat down in front of their television and listened to the news. And while they did that, they were busy cuddling one another. They decided to have a short prayer together before they went to bed, got under the quilt, kissed, and slept. And when he got up in the early hours of the morning to urinate, he tapped her and they started romancing and ended up having sexual intercourse before they slept again.

Chapter Nine: Day 9 – Monday

Positive communication in marriage

Mr and Mrs Evans are determined to build their marriage in a godly way. Hence, they always wake up to start thanking and praising God for His mercy to make it possible for them to wake up alive and well. Psalm 118:24 says this is the day the Lord has made, we will rejoice and be glad in it. They love this scripture and they do what it says by rejoicing and being glad daily. They prayed and settled down for their daily ministration.

PRISCILLA: Honey, I would like you to teach on the topic:

POSITIVE COMMUNICATION IN MARRIAGE

BARRY: He cleared his throat and started, "Positive communication in marriage is very important in order to maintain peace and progress. Let me start by saying here that we have various ways a couple can effectively communicate in marriage which includes talking, gestures, physical contact, writing, telephone and so on. It's important to use the best form of communication in any given situation, so that the receiver can correctly decode what the sender is saying. You must also avoid the use of jargon, swearing, and offensive words. Positive communication involves being polite, honest, true, and open-minded with your partner. Also, for communication to be effective, you must avoid barriers like noise, jargon, involving a third party, and the use of the wrong method. The essence of positive communication is to simplify the message enough for the receiver to understand what you are saying. Communication is therefore incomplete if the receiver does not understand the sender.

Communication is super complete when you say things and do what you say. That's called integrity. You will be causing offense if you say things to your partner and don't do it. You will appear to be a liar or be a liar if you do this, and your partner will lose confidence and trust in your words and that's unhealthy for the marriage. For example, couples must ensure they remain faithful to their marriage vows. Our God is a faithful God. He is forever committed to fulfilling His words, and as children of God created in His own image we must also ensure we fulfill our promises. Let your yea be yea, and nay be nay. Say what you mean, and mean what you say.

Perhaps I have to mention at this point that the use of certain words like *Always* or *Never* should not be used in the negative sense in marriage. Examples are: You always snore. You are always late to pick me up. You always come back home late. You are always dirty. You never help me. You never buy me clothes and jewellery. You never help me cook. You never help the children do their homework.

It's much better to replace *Always* and *Never* in a negative way with words like *Sometimes* or *Occasionally*.

They sound much more pleasant, true, and honest. For example, you sometimes snore. You are sometimes late to pick me. You sometimes come back home late etc.

On the other hand, it is perfectly alright to use always or never in a positive way. For example, you always pick me up early. You always come back home early. You are always clean. You always help me etc. Let us look at some scriptures below on communication.

Ephesians 4:29

> [29]*Let no corrupt communication proceed out of your mouth, but that which is good to the use of edifying, that it may minister grace unto the hearers.*

Examples of corrupt communication includes: You fucking bitch. You are a smelly pig. You are an asshole. You are a harlot. You are a dog. You are a bloody liar. You are a lazy bastard. You are too fat, ugly, and useless. You can go to hell and burn to ashes. You are so daft and foolish. You have a stinking behavior or attitude. You are a witch or wizard. These are examples of very offensive, slanderous phrases and should never be used because they are indeed corrupt communication.

Colossians 4:6

> [6]*Let your speech be always with grace, seasoned with salt, that ye may know how ye ought to answer every man.*

Examples of speech with grace, and words seasoned with salt. I love you. You are so beautiful or handsome. You always look good. You are very healthy and strong.

You are always smartly dressed. I like your hairstyle. Your perfume smells nice. I like your makeup. You are simply the best. You are fearfully and wonderfully made. You have a very good physique. I admire and adore you always. You are very intelligent. You always motivate and inspire me.

Ephesians 4:15

> *15But speaking the truth in love, may grow up into him in all things, which is the head, even Christ:*

Speaking the truth in love requires the wisdom of God to communicate the truth to your partner without offense. It means for example, as a wife you have to recognise the fact that your husband is your head, and therefore, you ought to show respect by being polite rather than brawl to make your grievance known to him. We need to speak in a low tone, avoiding raising our voice or shouting as we speak to our loved ones. There has to be mutual respect for both parties. Speaking the truth in love also means to avoid exaggeration and lies, and using the Bible as acceptable standard to get things done, and resolve issues.

Proverbs 12:18

> *18There is that speaketh like the piercings of a sword: but the tongue of the wise is health.*

It's important for us to always speak words that will heal and not wound our partner in marriage. Examples of words that are like the piercing of a sword are: You are mentally derailed and mad. The devil will hack you down to death. Die and go to hell and blaze to ashes. You are a fucking asshole. These sorts of words wound your partner like a sword piercing the body and should never be used. We must indeed control our anger and tongue because words spoken without thinking can never be brought back once they have gone out of the mouth."

After his teaching on positive communication in marriage she said, "Well done honey for the wonderful message. However, I have one question to ask. The question is this:

WHAT SHOULD HAPPEN IF THERE IS A SERIOUS BREAKDOWN IN COMMUNICATION IN A MARRIAGE?"

Barry continued again and said, "The party at fault should apologise. And he went ahead and gave a teaching on the topic:

JUST SAY SORRY

Genuinely saying sorry happens to be the hardest thing to do for some people, but it shouldn't really be so. It's a true demonstration of the character of God that a person transgresses whether against God or fellow man and says sorry, and means it. This automatically helps to enable you to have a free mind as well as to be at peace with whoever you need to apologise to. Avoid pride. Avoid claiming to always be right. The peace of God that surpasses all understanding is even more precious than gold. When you are at peace with yourself and your partner, it opens unexplainable doors of progress and prosperity. And mind you, when you say sorry to your partner, it does not necessarily mean you are wrong. It simply means you want to be at peace with the person, and it is indeed the right thing to do. People have wronged me several times, and I still humbled myself for the sake of peace and said sorry to them.

THINGS TO KNOW ABOUT SAYING SORRY

1. Peace will reign. See Mathew. 5:9 - This makes you a true child of God.
2. You will avoid further argument.
3. You will help your spiritual life to remain strong by not allowing strife.
4. When you genuinely say sorry and the person you said sorry to will not accept your apology, leave them alone and move on with your life.
5. Remember, your apology may not be accepted if your tone does not convey genuine remorse and repentance. Therefore, say sorry and mean it.
6. Say sorry at the right time. Don't say sorry next month when you should say it now or today. When sorry is not said at the right time, it may be meaningless.
7. Note that it is better to do the right thing and avoid saying sorry. Your sorry may not be accepted if you are known to say sorry after doing the wrong thing deliberately.
8. Proud and wicked people don't say sorry. They hurt people and are not bothered. It's better not to join them.

9. To say sorry to people you offend is about sowing a good seed. People will also say sorry to you when they hurt you.
10. Try not to demand sorry or apologies from people who hurt you. You will not fully enjoy the pleasure of their apology when you demand it. Sorry should flow naturally from the heart of the person saying it in order for it to be meaningful.
11. Sorry can act as a healing balm to those you hurt, or those who are in pain. So say it.
12. Saying sorry can save your marriage and other relationships. So say it and save your relationship.
13. Remember, to say sorry will not reduce your dignity, instead it will increase it.
14. Take advantage of this message and say sorry to someone who deserves it.

One last point that needs to be discussed here is the fact that when some people are offended, they expect the offender to say sorry before they will forgive them. It shouldn't really be so. Forgive everyone who offends you even if they don't say sorry. It is for your own good that you forgive, and avoid carrying the weight of grudges about. Remember, we live in a world where some people blindly claim to be right even when they are wrong, and this sadly sometimes includes us."

When he finished the message she started smiling and clapping for her husband and said, "Well done darling. I'm so satisfied with your teaching on communication today because you have just preached what you practice. You are polite to me as your wife.

You don't use swear words to hurt my feelings, and you are always quick to say sorry when you are wrong."

He replied and said, "Thanks for the compliment darling."

She came close to him and held him and kissed him.

They started to get ready to go to the gym for their exercise. They got to the gym and went straight to the treadmill to run, after which they got on other machines to workout. They had to also join the aerobics class to do a bit of aerobics. After an hour and half, they left the gym activities and went into the swimming pool. They carried on at the swimming pool for another twenty minutes after which they finally got back to their suite and got ready to be at the restaurant.

They arrived for their breakfast very late today, almost midday. They helped themselves to full English breakfast. After their meal, they relaxed a while and went straight back to their suite. When they got back they put on their television and sat on the sofa and she said, "I am very tired honey. I need some good rest now."

"That's fine, rest," said Barry.

She got into the bed and slept. The gym activity was perhaps a bit much for her he thought.

And when she woke up, they got out their chess set and started playing. Barry played with a lot of concentration again and won the game again and again. And that made him happy. She said, "What's happening here today? For me to lose the game again and again is unthinkable."

He said, "I'm now the chess master," and started laughing.

"Well done! You've done well honey. Let's play one more time," said Priscilla. And when they played again she won and that made her happy.

They prepared and went down to the restaurant to eat. After their meal, they got back to the suite and put on their love songs, and they sang along and danced together. And she got out *Dom Perignon* Champagne with no alcohol and opened it and served for two. It turned into a mini-party for two as they began to enjoy their drink. It wasn't long before the track titled: A Whole New World by Aladdin / Peabo Bryson and Andrea Tessa began to play. They sang the lyrics of this song together romantically. For them, this fantastic honeymoon is a whole new world of paradise on earth that should be forever. They played Ellie Goulding – Love Me Like You Do; Ariana Grande – One Last Time; Adele – Rolling In The Deep; Whitney Houston – I Will Always Love You; Barry White – You're The First, The Last, My Everything; Madonna – La Isla Bonita; Marvin Gaye - Let's Get It On; Bob Marley – Is This Love; and Frank Sinatra – Fly Me To The Moon. This track was followed by Just The Two Of Us by Grover Washington Jr. and this got them spinning round and in a groovy mood as they began to kiss and fondle one another and they began to undress. He took off her top and her bra exposing her breasts and he began to suck them saying, "You are so sweet darling, and I love you."

She replied and said, "I love you too darling."

The fondling continued as they build up the mood to copulate. He took off the rest of her clothes and his own and they began to kiss more closing their eyes, and panting, and she held his penis and rubbed it down gently again and again and he got full erection and she positioned herself in a missionary style on the bed as he penetrated her and he started making love to her so intensely that she began to shout, "Yeah, please give it to me. More! Harder! I love you darling. You are simply the best." And that got Barry energised the more as he came on with full blast with more jerks speedily. This got them over the moon in this exciting honeymoon.

They got into the bathroom and had a bath and got into their nightwear sprayed a bit of their favourite perfumes and sat in front of the television. And he said, "That was a great party we just had. I enjoyed it."

"Me too," she replied.

Barry said, "Honey, we had to play secular songs today because we need to have fun on this honeymoon. In future, we will mainly play gospel songs that will build us up spiritually." And Priscilla replied and said, "I totally agree with you darling."

"That reminds me," says Barry, "There will be a special live Jazz band performance here in Champion 5-Star Hotel Auditorium on Friday night. We shall be there. I have already got tickets for two of us." And she held him and kissed him and said, "Thanks, you are fantastic, and I love you."

He replied and said, "You are welcome darling."

They carried on with their romantic conversation until late at night and got into the bed and slept off.

Chapter Ten: Day 10 – Tuesday

The role of a husband, and the role of a wife in marriage

They woke up this beautiful Tuesday morning feeling strong and refreshed. And as their custom is, they started the day by giving thanks and praise to the Most High God and rounding it up with a powerful prayer session. They now settled down to do their Bible Study for the day, and Priscilla asked him to teach on the role of a husband in a marriage. He cleared his throat and began.

THE ROLE OF A HUSBAND IN A MARRIAGE

The first thing you must understand about the position of the first husband, Adam, created by God, is that he was created to be the head, to lead, love, provide for, and protect his wife Eve. He is also in a position to make important decisions for the family because God gave him the wisdom to do this, even though it may appear not to be so to some wives who want to usurp authority. He was first created by God, and God formed the wife out of his own ribs. In any organisation, community, or nation, you will only find a head or leader. The same thing applies to families, the grass root of the society. God created the husband to be the head and leader. That's why God made it clear from the onset. The husband is to play the following roles in marriage.

1. THE HEAD AND LEADER

The husband is to head the home and lead the wife, while she is to follow. The scriptures below make this position clear.

1 Corinthians 11:3

> ³But I would have you know, that the head of every man is Christ; <u>and the head of the woman is the man</u>; and the head of Christ is God. (Underline mine)

Genesis 3:16

> ¹⁶Unto the woman he said, I will greatly multiply thy sorrow and thy conception; in sorrow thou shalt bring forth children; <u>and thy desire shall be to thy husband, and he shall rule over thee</u>. (Underline mine)

1 Timothy 1:12

> ¹²But I suffer not a woman to teach, <u>nor to usurp authority over the man</u>, but to be in silence. (Underline mine)

2. LOVE AND CHERISH HIS WIFE

The following scriptures urge husbands to love their wives and this has to be unconditional agape love of Jesus.

Ephesians 5:25

> ²⁵Husbands, love your wives, even as Christ also loved the church, and gave himself for it;

Colossians 3:19

> *[19]Husbands, love your wives, and be not bitter against them.*

Ecclesiastes 9:9

> *[9]Live joyfully with the wife whom thou lovest all the days of the life of thy vanity, which he hath given thee under the sun, all the days of thy vanity: for that is thy portion in this life, and in thy labour which thou takest under the sun.*

3. RESPECT AND PROTECT HIS WIFE

Respect should be mutual and reciprocal. Therefore, the husband has to respect the wife.

1 Peter 3:7

> *[7]Likewise, ye husbands, dwell with them according to knowledge, giving honour unto the wife, as unto the weaker vessel, and as being heirs together of the grace of life; that your prayers be not hindered.*

4. PROVIDE FOR THE WIFE AND CHILDREN

The husband has a responsibility to provide for the needs of the family in all ramifications.

1 Timothy 5:8

> *[8]But if any provide not for his own, and specially for those of his own house, he hath denied the faith, and is worse than an infidel.*

When he finished his ministration, she said, "Thank you honey for the teaching."

He replied, "You are welcome darling." And he asked her to also give a teaching on the role of a wife in a marriage. She cleared her throat and began.

THE ROLE OF A WIFE IN A MARRIAGE

It's very important to fully understand that as a wife, you are marrying a man to play a supportive role as a help meet and this means that you have to follow him submissively and respectfully. He is the head and leader and the wife is to follow. Let's look at some scriptures below to explain the role of a wife in marriage.

1. TO SUBMIT AND RESPECT THE HUSBAND

The issue of submission and respect for your husband is a commandment from the Lord, and therein lies the beauty of a wife. Your beauty disappears as a wife if you decide to go the way of disrespect and rebellion against your husband in order to usurp his authority. One thing I observed as a wife is that even when your husband relinquishes authority to you to lead him, you may not be able to lead him properly as it ought to be. You will end up messing up things because a wife was never originally designed by God to lead the husband. Try not to be the one to make decisions for your husband. Present whatever you have to say as a *suggestion* to him and let him be the one to make decisions. Interestingly, as bad as his decisions may appear to be, God has a way of honouring his genuine decisions.

Ephesians 5:22

22 Wives, submit yourselves unto your own husbands, as unto the Lord.

Colossians 3:18

18 Wives, submit yourselves unto your own husbands, as it is fit in the Lord.

1 Peter 3:1-3

1 Likewise, ye wives, be in subjection to your own husbands; that, if any obey not the word, they also may without the word be won by the conversation of the wives;

2 While they behold your chaste conversation coupled with fear.

3 Whose adorning let it not be that outward adorning of plaiting the hair, and of wearing of gold, or of putting on of apparel;

Ephesians 5:33 Amplified

However, let each man of you [without exception] love his wife as [being in a sense] his very own self; and let the wife see that she respects and reverences her husband [that she notices him, regards him, honours him, prefers him, venerates, and esteems him; and that she defers to him, praises him, and loves and admires him exceedingly].

Esther 1:20

[20]And when the king's decree which he shall make shall be published throughout all his empire, (for it is great,) <u>all the wives shall give to their husbands honour,</u> both to great and small. (Underline mine)

2. TO BUILD THE HOME

It is the responsibility of the wife to build the home and building the home entails doing a number of things including supporting your husband and children positively in all they do.

Proverbs 14:1

Every wise woman buildeth her house: but the foolish plucketh it down with her hands.

3. LOVE YOUR HUSBAND

The commandment of love is for all Christians and the Bible also specifically says wives should love their husbands in the scripture below.

Titus 2:4

That they may teach the young women to be sober, <u>to love their husbands,</u> to love their children, (Underline mine)

It's important that you marry a man because you love him and not because you need a man to provide for you financially, or because you feel you are getting too old for marriage, or because you got pregnant by him to trap him into marriage. I would also like to emphasise here that you should not marry a man you cannot submit to or respect. As a Christian, you ought to have agape unconditional love for your husband.

4. SATISFY YOUR HUSBAND SEXUALLY AND WITH GOOD FOOD

Men love sex and they are sexually active. It is therefore important that as a wife you have to step up the game and satisfy your husband sexually to avoid him looking out for alternative women out there to satisfy his sexual drive. Initiate romance, love, and sex sessions and fully participate spirit, soul, and body.

You have to also cook good food for your husband which will help nourish him and make him sexually virile to produce healthy children. Have a cookery book and prepare and give him variety of food that will satisfy him.

5. QUALITIES OF A VIRTUOUS WIFE – PROVERBS 31:10–31

The scripture below says it all, detailing the qualities a virtuous wife needs to possess. Every wise wife should strive to possess these excellent qualities in order to be the best wife to their husband.

PROVERBS 31:10-31

¹⁰Who can find a virtuous woman? for her price is far above rubies.

¹¹The heart of her husband doth safely trust in her, so that he shall have no need of spoil.

¹²*She will do him good and not evil all the days of her life.*

¹³*She seeketh wool, and flax, and worketh willingly with her hands.*

¹⁴*She is like the merchants' ships; she bringeth her food from afar.*

¹⁵*She riseth also while it is yet night, and giveth meat to her household, and a portion to her maidens.*

¹⁶*She considereth a field, and buyeth it: with the fruit of her hands she planteth a vineyard.*

¹⁷*She girdeth her loins with strength, and strengtheneth her arms.*

¹⁸*She perceiveth that her merchandise is good: her candle goeth not out by night.*

¹⁹*She layeth her hands to the spindle, and her hands hold the distaff.*

²⁰*She stretcheth out her hand to the poor; yea, she reacheth forth her hands to the needy.*

²¹*She is not afraid of the snow for her household: for all her household are clothed with scarlet.*

²²*She maketh herself coverings of tapestry; her clothing is silk and purple.*

²³*Her husband is known in the gates, when he sitteth among the elders of the land.*

²⁴*She maketh fine linen, and selleth it; and delivereth girdles unto the merchant.*

²⁵*Strength and honour are her clothing; and she shall rejoice in time to come.*

²⁶*She openeth her mouth with wisdom; and in her tongue is the law of kindness.*

²⁷*She looketh well to the ways of her household, and eateth not the bread of idleness.*

²⁸*Her children arise up, and call her blessed; her husband also, and he praiseth her.*

²⁹*Many daughters have done virtuously, but thou excellest them all.*

³⁰*Favour is deceitful, and beauty is vain: but a woman that feareth the* LORD, *she shall be praised.*

³¹*Give her of the fruit of her hands; and let her own works praise her in the gates.*

She highlighted the following points about Proverbs 31:10-31.

1. A virtuous woman is an excellent woman in every ramification. She is of great value. Have that in your consciousness and carry yourself with respect and dignity. See verse 10 above again.
2. Your husband trusts you, so don't betray that trust. See verse 11.
3. Do good and not evil to your husband all the days of your life. See verse 12.
4. She works willingly with her hands because she is not lazy and brings food from afar. See verse 13-14.
5. She rises early and gives food to her household including her maidens. See verse 15.

6. She sees a good land and buys it with her own money and plants crops for harvest. See verse 16.
7. She is a woman of great strength and also a good businesswoman. See verse 17-18.
8. She helps the poor and needy. See verse 20.
9. She is not afraid to go out and work in the snow because she is not lazy. See verse 21.
10. She makes clothes for herself. See verse 22.
11. Her husband is known at the gates or town hall because of the respect and support she gives to her husband. See verse 23.
12. She makes clothes and sells them to merchants. She has her own Boutique. See verse 24.
13. She speaks words of wisdom and she is kind to people. See verse 26.
14. She is not a lazy woman. See verse 27.
15. Her children and husband praises her for her excellence. See verse 27 -28.
16. She has fear of the Lord. See verse 30.

When she finished her ministration, he immediately started clapping for her in approval and said, "I love you honey. You have obviously preached what you practice. You are indeed a virtuous wife to me and that's why I can relate to this beautiful message you have preached. Thanks for being the best wife in the world."

She replied with a broad smile on her face, "You are welcome darling. Thanks for the compliments."

They held each other and had a sweet kiss and he said, "I love you more than words can say."

She replied and said, "I love you too darling."

On that note, the Bible Study for the day came to a close.

They started getting ready to take a bath. And he called out to her saying, "My virtuous darling, please join me in the bathroom."

She answered and said, "Yes my lord." He replied, "That sounds good, you know, my virtuous darling." And they started laughing. 1 Peter 3:6 tells us Sarah called Abraham lord. And they got into the bath after they finished washing their teeth and his shaving. Barry washed her body and she washed his body while they laughed and joked together, praising their lovely bodies. They got out of the bathroom, dressed up and made their way to the restaurant to have their breakfast.

After their breakfast, they went outside having a stroll as they wait for their tour coach to arrive. They liked the weather with light sunshine though still very cold. The coach arrives, and they got in and met the tour guide and they greeted and they drove off straight to Bellver Castle.

The Tour Guide gave them the history of the Bellver Castle saying, "*Castell de Bellver* or 'Bellver Castle' is a striking, completely round, fourteenth century citadel near Palma in Majorca. The Bellver Castle is located three kilometres from Palma's city centre and 112.6m above sea level, dominating the bay and a large part of the island of Majorca. The castle is set high on top of the bay of Palma. The Catalan name 'Castell de Bellver' means 'The castle with a lovely view.'

Construction of Castell de Bellver began in 1310 in a Gothic style and took about nine years to complete under the rule of King James II and it remains extremely well preserved. With three main towers centred on a pretty courtyard and a looming keep, Castell de Bellver is a great example of military advances of the time, particularly as this style of castle is fairly unusual in Spain.

The lower levels of Castell de Bellver have a history of their own, having acted as a prison. The most famous figures imprisoned at Castell de Bellver include the family of King James III.

Today, Castell de Bellver houses a museum of history (Museu de Mallorca), displaying objects ranging from ancient Roman artefacts through to Arab pottery and seventeenth century ceramics." [14-15]

They moved into the Castle and the tour guide took them around to the different areas of the famous Castle while explaining important parts and items in them. Interesting! When they finished their tour, they made their way back to their hotel restaurant to have their lunch.

After their lunch they went to their suite to relax. They changed their clothes, put on their television, and sat on the sofa to relax. While they were there in front of the television, they started feeling sleepy and moved into the bedroom and slept off till late in the evening.

They got up and went down to have a light dinner at the restaurant and had some drinks at the bar before going back to their suite. As soon as they got back to their suite, they had their bath and night prayers and went to bed.

Chapter Eleven: Day 11 – Wednesday

Ruth and Boaz

Today is a special day on their honeymoon holiday. Special because they plan to see the Serra de Tramuntana Mountain and have a go climbing it a bit. So they woke up and, as usual, they are feeling strong both physically and mentally. They got together and started thanking and praising God for a smooth night rest, and praying committing the whole day into God's hands while asking for His protection against any form of accident as they go to see and climb the mountain.

When they finished their prayers, they got ready for their Bible study while Priscilla ministers on love. "My teaching today is on the classic love story of Ruth and Boaz. Hopefully, we will also see the film later on today," she says. She started by reading the entire book of Ruth and now focused more on chapter three as given below.

RUTH AND BOAZ

RUTH CHAPTER 3

¹Then Naomi her mother in law said unto her, my daughter, shall I not seek rest for thee, that it may be well with thee?

²*And now is not Boaz of our kindred, with whose maidens thou wast? Behold, he winnoweth barley to night in the threshingfloor.*

³*Wash thyself therefore, and anoint thee, and put thy raiment upon thee, and get thee down to the floor: but make not thyself known unto the man, until he shall have done eating and drinking.*

⁴*And it shall be, when he lieth down, that thou shalt mark the place where he shall lie, and thou shalt go in, and uncover his feet, and lay thee down; and he will tell thee what thou shalt do.*

⁵*And she said unto her, all that thou sayest unto me I will do.*

⁶*And she went down unto the floor, and did according to all that her mother in law bade her.*

⁷*And when Boaz had eaten and drunk, and his heart was merry, he went to lie down at the end of the heap of corn: and she came softly, and uncovered his feet, and laid her down.*

⁸*And it came to pass at midnight, that the man was afraid, and turned himself: and, behold, a woman lay at his feet.*

⁹*And he said, Who art thou? And she answered, I am Ruth thine handmaid: spread therefore thy skirt over thine handmaid; for thou art a near kinsman.*

¹⁰*And he said, blessed be thou of the* LORD*, my daughter: for thou hast shewed more kindness in the*

latter end than at the beginning, inasmuch as thou followedst not young men, whether poor or rich.

¹¹*And now, my daughter, fear not; I will do to thee all that thou requirest: for all the city of my people doth know that thou art a virtuous woman.*

¹²*And now it is true that I am thy near kinsman: howbeit there is a kinsman nearer than I.*

¹³*Tarry this night, and it shall be in the morning, that if he will perform unto thee the part of a kinsman, well; let him do the kinsman's part: but if he will not do the part of a kinsman to thee, then will I do the part of a kinsman to thee, as the* LORD *liveth: lie down until the morning.*

¹⁴*And she lay at his feet until the morning: and she rose up before one could know another. And he said, Let it not be known that a woman came into the floor.*

¹⁵*Also he said, Bring the vail that thou hast upon thee, and hold it. And when she held it, he measured six measures of barley, and laid it on her: and she went into the city.*

¹⁶*And when she came to her mother in law, she said, Who art thou, my daughter? And she told her all that the man had done to her.*

¹⁷*And she said, these six measures of barley gave he me; for he said to me, Go not empty unto thy mother in law.*

¹⁸*Then said she, sit still, my daughter, until thou know how the matter will fall: for the man will not be in rest, until he have finished the thing this day.*

After reading the above chapter, she started highlighting some important points in this beautiful love story especially to encourage women. She says:

1. Ruth lost her husband and became a widow, but remained loyal to her mother-in-law, Naomi, and eventually found favour in the sight of the Lord and was divinely connected to her new husband, Boaz, through Naomi. This story shows that a wife should have a good relationship with her mother-in-law. Don't see your mother-in-law as a witch or a wicked evil person as some people do.

2. Naomi served as both a mother-in-law and a mentor to Ruth advising and guiding her on what to do in order to get hooked up with Boaz. When you have a good relationship with your mother-in-law, she can also be your mentor and guide you.

3. It's not only men that should always initiate or make the first move in a romance, love, and sex affair. A woman can also initiate it. Naomi advised Ruth in verse three above to, *"Wash thyself therefore, and anoint thee, and put thy raiment upon thee, and get thee down to the floor: but make not thyself known unto the man, until he shall have done eating and drinking."* According to this verse, to capture a man's attention, you need to have a good bath, anoint yourself or wear a good perfume, put on a good cloth, and meet a man when he is relaxing. Good tip for singles.

4. Note that you can be led as a single woman to initiate a romance with a man. This does not make you wayward, loose, or desperate. Ruth made the first move here. Read again what verses 7–9 says.

7And when Boaz had eaten and drunk, and his heart was merry, he went to lie down at the end of the heap of corn: and she came softly, and uncovered his feet, and laid her down.

8And it came to pass at midnight, that the man was afraid, and turned himself: and, behold, a woman lay at his feet.

9And he said, Who art thou? And she answered, I am Ruth thine handmaid: spread therefore thy skirt over thine handmaid; for thou art a near kinsman.

There has to be a period for searching out of the person you are about to marry. Ask questions and investigate matters of interest regarding the person and the family you intend to be married into. For example, Boaz had to enquire if he was the nearest kinsman to marry Ruth.

When she finished the ministration, Barry said, "That's a lovely message sweetheart."

She replied, "Thanks darling."

They started getting ready to go for the tour of the Serra de Tramuntana Mountain. When they were ready they went to the restaurant to have their breakfast before they set off. They waited for their coach briefly and when it turned up they drove off.

When they got there, the Tour Guide started giving them information about the mountain saying, "The *Serra de Tramuntana* is a range of mountain that runs along the northwest coast of Majorca. With a length of 90 km and a width of 15km at some points, it includes 18 municipalities and covers about 30% of the island's territory.

In 2011, the mountain range was declared a UNESCO World Heritage Site in the cultural landscape category. The Serra de Tramuntana definitely deserves a visit during your Majorca holidays.

UNESCO declared the area a place of 'World Heritage' because of its outstanding value to humanity. Mankind has been able to adapt to a land devoid of water by engineering a water-channelling system of Arab origin, ultimately transforming the landscape. The Serra de Tramuntana mountain range is a Mediterranean Agricultural landscape; it is characterised by terraces, water mills and dry-stone buildings, and planted with olive trees, almond trees, oranges, tomatoes, and vines.

The highest peak is the Puig Major, which, at 1,445 metres is the highest mountain in the Balearic Islands. It is closely followed by the Puig de Massanella, which stands at 1,364 metres.

The climate in the Tramuntana Range is significantly wetter than the rest of the island, recording as much as 1,507mm (59.3 inches) of precipitation per year, in comparison with some other parts of the island where annual rainfall is less than 400mm (15 inches). It is also cooler due to the height and a few days of snow are not unusual during winter. It has some of the most beautiful towns in the whole of Majorca. These are being Valldemossa, Banyalbufar, Deia, Soller, Estellencs, Fornalutx and, of course, Pollença. The Serra de Na Burguesa is the southernmost portion of the Tramuntana Range.

The MA10 road runs through the entire Serra, from Andratx to Pollença, crossing vertiginous landscapes, where unexpected cliffs overlook the sea. The colours of the landscape change depending on the season. Sometimes the peaks are covered with snow in winter, and the towns have the enchantment of a typical mountain village. It's no coincidence that these views have inspired many internationally renowned artists in their creative work.

One of the best ways to explore is, therefore, by car. The beautiful capital of La Palma is a great place to start, but from any corner of the island you can reach the Serra quickly. Ideally, the trip can be done along the MA10 in three days, enough time to get to know the entirety of this wonder."[16-18]

They wanted to have a go and climb a bit of the mountain, but the tour guide strongly advised against that because it's winter time and there is snow and ice, which makes the surfaces slippery and dangerous to climb. Though they were disappointed not to climb, health and safety is also of paramount importance to them. They pulled out their cameras and mobile phones and took pictures of the beautiful nature on the mountain. The rocks, plants, heaps of snow, and the blue sky all reveal the handiwork of God. After seeing the glory of the mountains, they acknowledged that God is indeed great and supreme in His creation.

They came back to the hotel and went straight to the restaurant to have their lunch. After having their delicious meal, they went back to their suite to relax. After relaxing for a while, they decided to see the film about Ruth and Boaz to conclude their morning ministration. She downloaded the film from the internet, and they settled down and watched the film as they enjoy a bottle of red wine. Reading the entire book of

Ruth earlier in the morning helped them to understand and fully enjoy the film. It's indeed an interesting biblical story of romance, love, and family. After the film, they went down to the restaurant and had their dinner. They said their night prayer after relaxing, and had their bath and went to bed.

Chapter Twelve: Day 12 – Thursday

The fear of the Lord in marriage

They woke up feeling great. As usual, they commenced the day by singing praises unto the Lord and praying. After that, they proceeded to do their Bible Study for the day. Priscilla commenced ministration and delivered teaching on the topic:

THE FEAR OF THE LORD

Psalms 111:10

> *¹The fear of the Lord is the beginning of wisdom: a good understanding have all they that do his commandments: his praise endureth forever."*

To fear God does not mean you have to start running away from God because He will bully you and punish you. No! God loves you. He is your Father. We are talking about reverential fear here, and this simply means to know His Word and respect Him by obeying His Word. To fear God also means to detest sin, and also desist from doing anything you believe will make Him angry. Take for example, you have your earthly biological father, who you live with and you know those things he doesn't like, and you avoid doing them. Similarly, don't do anything the Bible says you shouldn't do because God will not like it.

Psalms 119:11

> *"Thy word have I hid in mine heart, that I might not sin against thee."*

Flood your heart with scriptures, so much that whenever there is an issue to deal with, you already have a scripture addressing that issue. Let the Word of God hid in your heart counsel you always. Anytime you know what the Word of God says, and you fail to obey it, you don't fear Him. Again, you don't fear God if you only do the right things because people are watching you. The fear of God means that you do the right things even when no one is watching you in your secret chambers. God is watching you anyway because His presence is everywhere. God knows those who fear Him and He rewards them. You can't fake the fear of God.

THE FEAR OF THE LORD IN MARRIAGE

When you truly have the fear of the Lord as a born-again Christian, filled with the Holy Spirit, with evidence of speaking in tongues, and full of the Word of God, there are certain things you will not do to your partner because you fear God. For example, if you truly fear God,

> You will study the Bible, obey it, pray, praise and worship God at all times.
> You will love your partner.
> You will submit to your husband.
> You will be honest with your partner.
> You will have respect for your partner.

You will always agree with your partner.
You will live in peace with your partner.
You will not commit adultery.
You will not be abusive to your partner.
You will not engage in lies in your marriage.
You will not deny your partner sex.
You will not defraud your partner in any way.

BENEFITS OF THE FEAR OF THE LORD

1. THE FEAR OF GOD WILL REVEAL HIS SECRET TO YOU.

Psalms 25:14

"The secret of the Lord is with them that fear him; and he will shew them his covenant."

2. IT WILL PROLONG YOUR DAYS.

Proverbs 10:27

"The fear of the Lord prolongeth days: but the years of the wicked shall be shortened."

3. IT WILL BRING FORTH RICHES

Proverbs 22:4

"By humility and the fear of the Lord are riches, and honour, and life." God will reward you with riches, honour, and life when you fear Him. See also Genesis 22:16-18.

4. CONCLUSION OF THE WHOLE MATTER

Ecclesiastes 12:13

> *Let us hear the conclusion of the whole matter: fear God, and keep his commandments: for this is the whole duty of man.*

God bless you in Jesus' name. Amen!"

After the ministration by Priscilla, he said, "That's a great message you have just given, darling, and I'm truly blessed."

She smiled and said, "Thanks honey."

They started getting ready to have their bath, and as they did that they started talking about their cruise for the day. The *ship cruise* is scheduled to last for two hours and it's meant to help them have sightseeing from the sea of most parts of the Island of Majorca.

"It's going to be exciting," said Barry.

Priscilla replied, "I know. I haven't been on a ship before so it's indeed going to be exciting."

"I haven't been on a ship before either," Barry replied.

They started laughing as they washed one another's bodies in the Jacuzzi, and she jokingly said, "Will you position yourself well you little boy so that I can wash you well?"

They laughed as he replied, "Alright Mummy," and they laughed all the more.

After they dressed up and got ready they first went down to the restaurant to have their breakfast. They had their delicious English breakfast and relaxed very well as they waited for the coach to arrive for their cruise.

The coach arrived and they set off to Port Alcudia where they will take the cruise ship. There are so many planned cruise rides and from various points on the Island organised by different operators but they have chosen Broadway cruise operators because of their proven record for excellent services. They also have the Mallorca North Coast Catamaran Cruise. The Broadway cruise has planned routes north, south, east, and west of the island. They chose the north and the itinerary includes the following locations: Port Alcudia, Port Pollensa, Cala San Vicente, Playa de Muro, and Can Picafort.

When they got to the beautiful ship they were briefly conducted round and instructed on health and safety measures. The beauty of the ship left them in awe as they quietly stared at parts of the ship in admiration.

The cruise on the Mediterranean Sea gives a good view along the coast of Majorca from the luxurious vessel, allowing you to see the rocks and impressive natural features on the island along with the beautiful green vegetation of the island and also breathe refreshing unpolluted sea air. While on the cruise, they were treated to a buffet with a wide-ranging intercontinental menu, along with assorted drinks and fruits. They had the chance to be together and talk. They were offered the chance to participate in snorkelling but they chose not to. They enjoyed their cruise with lovely conversations until they got back to their hotel suite. Being tired, they went to have a nap. They woke up and had their dinner.

They have a special live Spanish Jazz musical performance coming up tomorrow at the hotel auditorium by popular international musician Eddie Santiago and they are looking forward to it. They talked about it briefly with excitement, prayed and retired to bed.

Chapter Thirteen: Day 13 – Friday

Samson and Delilah; &
Spanish jazz concert

They woke up early in the morning and said their prayers as usual, committing the day into God's hands for peace and protection. After their morning devotion, they went into the Jacuzzi and had their bath. They dressed up and went down to the restaurant for their breakfast and went from there to do their shopping, as they are due to leave Palma for Edinburgh tomorrow.

After their delicious breakfast and brief relaxation, they set off to do some shopping for souvenirs and clothing at the *Centro Commercial Porto Pi shopping complex*. Priscilla said, "I would like to have some clothes, shoes and bags."

Barry replied, "You are *always* getting more clothes, shoes, and bags."

She said, "Always? Remember you preached against the use of the words 'never' and 'always' in a negative way."

"I'm sorry. You *sometimes* get more clothes, shoes, and bags." He corrected himself.

"That's a better way to communicate darling," replied Priscilla.

"It was a slip of tongue," Barry said, giggling.

As they got to the beautiful shopping complex, they went into the souvenir shops to get some. They looked into the Boutiques to buy some female dresses, shoes, and bags and they found some nice items and the prices were quite reasonable, as they compare the exchange rate of Pounds Sterling with Euro currency. She picked the following items: *CeliaB dress; Louis Vuitton* bag; *Dolce & Gabbana* perfume, shoe and bag; and *Valentino San Gallo* dress for special occasions, and Barry paid for them.

She said after Barry had paid, "Thanks a million sweetheart, you are a blessing to me and I appreciate you. I love you."

Barry replied, "You are welcome darling."

The amount he paid was nothing compared to the huge amounts he used to spend on shopping for Anna Murray, his ex-girlfriend. He is glad it's all over with Anna Murray now. Barry only got a few *Gucci* and *Dior* T-shirts and undies for himself.

They finished their shopping and went back to the hotel. And after a while, they went to the restaurant to have their lunch. While having their lunch, they started talking about the special *Spanish Jazz live musical performance* coming up tonight at the hotel auditorium by popular international musician Eddie Santiago and they are excited about it.

She said, "We will get our clothes ready for the show now."

Barry replied, "My clothes are ready. You are the one that needs to get your clothes ready."

They finished their meal and went back to their suite and she got her clothes for the show ready. The show will start at 8 pm and finish by 10 pm, which is fine as they are due to vacate their suite by midday tomorrow. That gives them enough time to sleep and get ready.

They did not do their Bible Study in the morning. So they decided to do it now. Barry suggested the story of Samson and Delilah, and for them to also see the film. She agreed to that and Barry commenced his ministration to her by reading the entire *Judges 16* as follows:

"¹Then went Samson to Gaza, and saw there an harlot, and went in unto her.

²And it was told the Gazites, saying, Samson is come hither. And they compassed him in, and laid wait for him all night in the gate of the city, and were quiet all the night, saying, In the morning, when it is day, we shall kill him.

³And Samson lay till midnight, and arose at midnight, and took the doors of the gate of the city, and the two posts, and went away with them, bar and all, and put them upon his shoulders, and carried them up to the top of an hill that is before Hebron.

⁴And it came to pass afterward, that <u>he loved a woman</u> in the valley of Sorek, whose name was <u>Delilah</u>.

⁵<u>And the lords of the Philistines came up unto her,</u> and said unto her, Entice him, and see wherein his great strength lieth, and by what means we may prevail against him, that we may <u>bind him to afflict him</u>; and we will give thee every one of us <u>eleven hundred pieces of silver.</u>

⁶And Delilah said to Samson, tell me, I pray thee, wherein thy great strength lieth, and wherewith thou mightest be bound to afflict thee.

⁷*And Samson said unto her, if they bind me with seven green withs that were never dried, then shall I be weak, and be as another man.*

⁸*Then the lords of the Philistines brought up to her seven green withs which had not been dried, and she bound him with them.*

⁹*Now there were men lying in wait, abiding with her in the chamber. And she said unto him, The Philistines be upon thee, Samson. And he brake the withs, as a thread of tow is broken when it toucheth the fire. So his strength was not known.*

¹⁰*And Delilah said unto Samson, Behold, thou hast mocked me, and told me lies: now tell me, I pray thee, wherewith thou mightest be bound.*

¹¹*And he said unto her, if they bind me fast with new ropes that never were occupied, then shall I be weak, and be as another man.*

¹²*Delilah therefore took new ropes, and bound him therewith, and said unto him, The Philistines be upon thee, Samson. And there were liers in wait abiding in the chamber. And he brake them from off his arms like a thread.*

¹³*And Delilah said unto Samson, hitherto thou hast mocked me, and told me lies: tell me wherewith thou mightest be bound. And he said unto her, If thou weavest the seven locks of my head with the web.*

¹⁴*And she fastened it with the pin, and said unto him, The Philistines be upon thee, Samson. And he*

awaked out of his sleep, and went away with the pin of the beam, and with the web.

¹⁵*And she said unto him, how canst thou say, I love thee, when thine heart is not with me? thou hast mocked me these three times, and hast not told me wherein thy great strength lieth.*

¹⁶<u>*And it came to pass, when she pressed him daily with her words, and urged him, so that his soul was vexed unto death;*</u>

¹⁷<u>*That he told her all his heart, and said unto her,*</u> *there hath not come a razor upon mine head; for I have been a Nazarite unto God from my mother's womb: if I be shaven, then my strength will go from me, and I shall become weak, and be like any other man.*

¹⁸*And when Delilah saw that he had told her all his heart, she sent and called for the lords of the Philistines, saying, come up this once, for he hath shewed me all his heart. Then the lords of the Philistines came up unto her, and brought money in their hand.*

¹⁹*And she made him sleep upon her knees; and she called for a man, and she caused him to shave off the seven locks of his head; and she began to afflict him, and his strength went from him.*

²⁰*And she said, the Philistines be upon thee, Samson. And he awoke out of his sleep, and said, I will go out as at other times before, and shake myself. And he wist not that the* LORD *was departed from him.*

²¹*But the Philistines took him, and put out his eyes, and brought him down to Gaza, and bound him with fetters of brass; and he did grind in the prison house.*

²²*Howbeit the hair of his head began to grow again after he was shaven.*

²³*Then the lords of the Philistines gathered them together for to offer a great sacrifice unto Dagon their god, and to rejoice: for they said, our god hath delivered Samson our enemy into our hand.*

²⁴*And when the people saw him, they praised their god: for they said, our god hath delivered into our hands our enemy, and the destroyer of our country, which slew many of us.*

²⁵*And it came to pass, when their hearts were merry, that they said, call for Samson, that he may make us sport. And they called for Samson out of the prison house; and he made them sport: and they set him between the pillars.*

²⁶*And Samson said unto the lad that held him by the hand, suffer me that I may feel the pillars whereupon the house standeth, that I may lean upon them.*

²⁷*Now the house was full of men and women; and all the lords of the Philistines were there; and there were upon the roof about three thousand men and women, that beheld while Samson made sport.*

²⁸*And Samson called unto the* LORD, *and said, O Lord God, remember me, I pray thee, and strengthen me, I pray thee, only this once, O God, that I may be at once avenged of the Philistines for my two eyes.*

²⁹*And Samson took hold of the two middle pillars upon which the house stood, and on which it was*

borne up, of the one with his right hand, and of the other with his left.

30 And Samson said, let me die with the Philistines. And he bowed himself with all his might; and the house fell upon the lords, and upon all the people that were therein. So the dead which he slew at his death were more than they which he slew in his life.

31 Then his brethren and all the house of his father came down, and took him, and brought him up, and buried him between Zorah and Eshtaol in the burying place of Manoah his father. And he judged Israel twenty years. (Underline mine)

When he finished reading the entire chapter, he continued by highlighting the following points:

LESSONS FOR MEN:

1. The Bible says in verse 4 above that Samson loved Delilah, and the same woman he loved betrayed him into the hands of the Philistines, his enemies. This is very similar to the Judas betrayal of Jesus. Jesus loved Judas with agape love, yet Judas betrayed Him for just 30 pieces of silver after Satan had entered him. Here, we also see Delilah in verse 5 and 18 being offered 1,100 pieces of silver to betray Samson. Who can you trust? Delilah's actions clearly show Satan may have also entered her for her to accept bribe to betray a man who loved her. This is heartbreaking! Funny enough, we still see such betrayals from women today in relationships. This story teaches men to be careful because even

your loved ones can betray you. After all, the Bible says in **Matthew 10:36** that, *"And a man's foes shall be they of his own household."*

2. The Bible says in *1 Corinthians 13:8 of NIV, "Love never fails…"* However, each time I read about how Jesus loved Judas and he betrayed Him, and how Samson loved Delilah and she betrayed him, I am tempted to question the effectiveness of love. To suffer and die as a result of the betrayal of a loved one is painful. The only thing I can say here is that Jesus was meant to die for the sins of the whole world and it was in God's plan that He should be betrayed by Judas before death and nothing could stop that divine plan. On the other hand, I would like to believe that perhaps Samson was successfully betrayed by Delilah because he had erotic and philanthropic love for her rather than agape love which is much more effective. Agape love never fails, but erotic and philanthropic love could fail.

3. Perhaps Samson was even foolish to have disclosed to Delilah where his strength lies for him to be afflicted, but when you come to think of the fact that love trusts, you may not really blame him for eventually disclosing it. See verse 6 and 15.

4. Looking at this story, and how Samson disclosed where his strength lies to the one he loved and died, I believe it serves as a lesson to know that such disclosure should not include anything that can lead to death. You must apply wisdom and withhold such information except you want to die. Samson violated the commandment of God that he should not allow razor to come on his head. See verse 17

above and also Judges 13:5. Why should Samson breach such a rule? Disobedience! The protocol for the consecration of his power is a secret. Not even love for Delilah should have made him disclose the source of his strength.

5. The climax of this story is verse 16, which tells us that Delilah pressed Samson daily with her words and urged him so much that his soul was vexed unto death. You must deal with any situation that threatens your life and don't treat it with levity. Seek help fast because that might be Delilah seeking to kill you. Delilah is indeed wicked."

After he finished the teaching, he noticed that she wasn't happy because Delilah is a woman like her, and she did that to Samson, her loved one. She now said to Barry, "I can't argue with the truth in the Bible. The message is good and it should serve as a lesson to both men and women because what happened to Samson could have happened to Delilah. Men do betray and kill their wives or loved ones as well."

"That's true," said Barry. He continued and said, "That's a good contribution and remark darling."

Priscilla said, "Honey, I would like you to be at rest. I am not a Delilah. I will not betray or kill you. I love you spirit, soul, and body. I have to say this to reassure you because I saw the looks on your face suggesting fear as you gave the teaching." She stood up and held Barry and said, "I love you honey," and kissed him.

"I love you too," he said, and they laughed it all off.

She immediately downloaded the Samson and Delilah film from the internet and they began to watch and because they read the biblical account before watching the film, it helped their understanding of the film. They went on and watched the film and when God answered Samson's prayer to strengthen him one more time because of his eyes that were put out, and he pulled down the pillars of the building killing thousands, they were deeply touched.

Afterwards, they had their bath and got dressed. Barry put on a Dolce & Gabbana Tuxedo suit, and she wore her Valentino San Gallo black dress with little white design, a beautiful golden necklace and pendant, earrings, bracelet, with her nicely done hair, shoes, bag, and used *Estee Lauder* makeup to match. They also topped it up with their lovely perfumes.

"You are beautiful and gorgeously dressed sweetheart," says Barry.

"Thank you honey," she said as he held her and gave her a kiss. And she said again, "Thank you honey."

And they went down to the restaurant to have their dinner before the show started.

As they began to make their way down to the restaurant to have their dinner they noticed that there were quite a number of people at the hotel, and they were smartly dressed, obviously for the show. The whole atmosphere at the Champion Hotel has changed and people are gathered together in small groups talking about Eddie Santiago show coming up tonight.

They served their meal and ate while enjoying the Eddie Santiago music being played at the restaurant. A foretaste of what is going to happen tonight. That began to hype up their feelings and expectations as they keenly looked forward to the show to start, for them to dance and enjoy. Out of curiosity he asked the restaurant manager if there would be a chance for people to also dance in the auditorium, and he said yes, and that made him happy as he wants to dance with his wife during the live Jazz musical performance.

They left the restaurant at 7.45pm and went down to the auditorium to find a long queue at the entrance door. Their tickets were checked and they were cleared and allowed to go in. And as they got in, it was 8 pm and time to start the show. It was a massive auditorium with beautiful lighting, artworks, and decoration and a massive centre stage with various musical instruments on display. The auditorium is almost full to its maximum capacity of 3,000 persons. The announcer took the microphone on the stage and said, "Señoras y señores, el espectáculo está a punto de comenzar y me gustaría presentarles el músico de Jazz internacional Eddie Santiago y su super grupo de banda de Jazz." Meaning, "Ladies and Gentlemen, the show is about to start and I would like to introduce to you the international Jazz musician Eddie Santiago and his super Jazz band."

They all came on stage in a grand style and took their places while the whole audience stood up clapping with roars of approval and people were chanting, "Eddie! Eddie!! Eddie!!!" The feeling is great.

Eddie took the microphone and said, "Ciudad de Palma, es genial estar aquí esta noche. Te amo todos." Meaning, "Palma city, it's great to be here tonight. I love you all," and he took his place on the keyboard and the show started. He played many special numbers including: My Love For You Will Never Die; Teach Me How To Love You; Jamboree Time; Kiss Me All Over; Abracadabra; Touch Me; and This Honeymoon Will Last Forever. All the songs were played in Spanish.

As Eddie and his band played, the whole audience was drawn into wild excitement with cheers, singing, clapping, and dancing. This was the first time they saw a live Spanish jazz performance, and they were really thrilled. A few times, Mr and Mrs Evans joined in the singing, clapping and dancing. It was a solid two hours of non-stop live music performance. Two hours went so fast and the show was brought to a close by the announcer as he grabbed the microphone and said, "Señoras y señores, quisiera anunciar a las dos horas de actuación de música en vivo de Eddie Santiago que lamentablemente el programa está llegando a su fin ahora. Gracias por asistir y buenas noches." Meaning, "Ladies and Gentlemen, I would like to announce after two hours of live music performance by Eddie Santiago that sadly the show is coming to an end now. Thanks for attending, and good night." The audience started clapping their hands, and gradually began to leave the hall.

Mr and Mrs Evans left and went back to their suite. They quickly undressed and had their shower and sat in front of the television to relax as they talk about the show. Barry said, "I loved every bit of that show, mainly because it was Jazz and also Spanish. It makes a huge difference to have something Spanish." And in her usual manner of supporting her husband she said, "Honey, I also love it for the same reason." And she continued and said, "Thanks for the outing darling. This is indeed an exciting honeymoon surprise show. The memory will live with me forever." And he replied and said, "You are welcome honey." It wasn't long and they got together for a short prayer after which they went to bed, kissed, and slept.

Chapter Fourteen: Day 14 – Saturday

Journey back to Edinburgh

They woke up feeling great and, as their usual custom, they started praising and thanking God and they prayed. Today is the last day of their honeymoon at the Champion 5-star hotel. So their thanksgiving and praise was intense for a time well spent at the hotel. They thanked God for His protection, provisions, and for giving them the power to enjoy their honeymoon. They also prayed for a smooth and safe flight back to Edinburgh.

After their morning devotion, they started packing their things gradually as they are due to vacate their hotel suite by midday. Meanwhile, they played their love songs and sang along. They got out all their clothes and shoes from the wardrobe and packed them. After packing, they held one another and started caressing and kissing and made love so intensely for the final time in this Champion 5-star hotel paradise where they had their memorable honeymoon. They went into the bathroom and had their bath and dressed smartly and made sure they are not leaving anything behind by double-checking the side drawers, tables, wardrobe, and bathroom. They went down to the restaurant and had their breakfast and when they finished, they got out to the reception to officially check out. And they met Samantha who greeted them and asked in Spanish, "¿Espero que tuvieras un buen tiempo aquí con nosotros?" Meaning, "I hope you had a nice time here with us?"

They answered together, "Sí" Meaning "Yes!"

Samantha went ahead and officially checked them out. And Antonio was already there to take them to Palma de Mallorca Airport from where they will board a flight back to Edinburgh. They got into the car and he took them to the airport.

They quickly went to the departure section and checked in their luggage and confirmed their flight. This is passenger Airbus A320 with flight N0. 3335. While they waited to board the flight, she said, "This honeymoon went so fast, the two weeks is like two minutes to me."

He started laughing and said, "I know. I feel the same way." They wished the honeymoon had continued at the Champion Hotel for much longer.

They boarded the plane and fastened their seat belts and began to share their beautiful experiences and enjoyment in the wonderful island. They talked about the romantic love sessions and laughed together. They talked about their tour of the different landmarks, gym workouts, romantic movies they watched, and the prayer and Bible Study teachings. Everything is just brilliant and exciting. They are so satisfied with the trip and agreed that they will revisit the island again in the future. As they talked, the pilot began to announce that everyone should fasten their seat belts because they were about to start descending to land in Edinburgh Airport shortly.

"Oh my God, we are already in Edinburgh," Priscilla gasped.

Barry checked his Rolex wristwatch and said, "The time goes so fast. We are due to touch down now indeed."

They arrived safely and drove back to their home in a cab. They are determined to make their marriage work and this requires effort, commitment, investment, and sacrifice from both parties. To help them achieve this, they are determined to follow the blueprint of goals that they wrote down, which of course is subject to regular reviews.

Three weeks after their return to Edinburgh she missed her menstrual cycle, and they went ahead and had a bouncing baby boy exactly nine months from their memorable honeymoon. They have joy, and their joy is indeed full and overflowing. They are both radiant and flourishing with amazing grace in abundance, full of love, peace, and joy in this blissful marriage.

Finally, we see here that Mr and Mrs Evans had just a two-week honeymoon. And **Deuteronomy 24:5** that was referred to earlier says a man should take one full year off cheering up his new wife on a honeymoon. But King Solomon takes it further by stating that a honeymoon should be everyday forever for a couple. This is how he put it in **Ecclesiastics 9:9**, "*Live joyfully with the wife whom thou lovest all the days of the life of thy vanity, which he hath given thee under the sun, all the days of thy vanity: for that is thy portion in this life, and in thy labour which thou takest under the sun.*" To live joyfully with your lovely wife all the days of your life simply implies everyday honeymoon forever. Enjoy honeymoon every day forever in Jesus' name. Amen!

SPREAD THE GOOD NEWS

Well done! You have successfully finished reading this book. I believe you must have picked up some principles that will help you grow in the Word of God, and spiritually as you apply them in your life. It is the application of the principles you have learnt that will bring about a transformation in your life and also give you your desired results. So, keep on practicing what you have learnt.

Now that you have read this book, and you are blessed, I would like you to tell your family, friends, and colleagues about it and spread the good news of the principles you have learnt. Recommend this book to at least twenty people you know, and you can even get some copies for your loved ones as a gift. As you do this, you become a blessing to others and also enlighten the world from where you are. Thank you and God bless you abundantly.

MICHAEL NWADUBA

BIBLIOGRAPHY

1. The Holy Bible containing the Old and New Testaments. Authorized King James Version. Reference Edition. Thomas Nelson Bibles, A Division of Thomas Nelson Inc. Copyright 1989 Thomas Nelson Inc. Printed in the United States of America.
2. The Living Bible. Parents Resource Bible. A Life Application Bible. Edysyl Publications. Parents Resource Bible. Copyright 1995 by Tyndale House Publishers.
3. The Amplified Bible. Copyright 1954, 1958, 1962, 1964, 1965, 1987, by The Lockman Foundation.
4. The Thompson Chain-Reference Study Bible. Second Improved Edition. New International Version. Copyright 1973, 1978, 1984 by International Bible Society.
5. Heward-Mills, Dag. *Model Marriage: A Marriage Counselling Handbook*. Parchment House. 2005.

NOTES

1. Jose Feliciano: Feliz Navidad –https://www.google. co.uk/search?q=feliz+navidad+lyrics&oq=FELIZ+ NAVIDAD+ LYRICS&aqs=chrome.0.0l6.9719j1j 4&sourceid=chrome&ie=UTF-8 (Accessed 8 May, 2018).
2. Sex positions – https://www.menshealth.com/sex-women/45-sex-positions-guys-should-know – (Accessed October 5, 2017).
3. Palma Cathedral – http://www.northsouthguides. com/mallorca_cathedral.html – (Accessed 5 October, 2017).
4. Royal Palace of La Almudaina – https://en.wikipedia. org/wiki/Royal_Palace_of_La_Almudaina – (Accessed 5 October, 2017).
5. Palacio real de la Almudaina –http://www.spainis culture.com/en/monumentos/mallorca/palacio_real_ de_la_almudaina.html - (Accessed 5 October, 2017).
6. 10 tips for a healthy functioning penis – http:// www.privategym.com/blog/10-tips-for-a-healthy-functioning-penis – (Accessed 5 October, 2017).
7. How to care for your vulva —https://www.google. co.uk/search?q=how+to+care+for+your+vulva&ie =utf-8&oe=utf-8&client=firefox-b&gfe_rd=cr& dcr=0&ei=qLjWWceIDsH38AeYx4vwCQ___- (Accessed 5 October, 2017).

8. James Cameron: Titanic film 1997 – https://en.wikipedia.org/wiki/Titanic_(1997_film) – (Accessed 5 October, 2017).

9. William Shakespeare: Romeo and Juliet – https://en.wikipedia.org/wiki/Romeo_and_Juliet - (Accessed 5 October, 2017)

10. William Shakespeare: Romeo and Juliet – https://simple.wikipedia.org/wiki/Romeo_and_Juliet – (Accessed 5 October, 2017).

11. John Assaraf: How to set and achieve goals' video – http://www.bing.com/search?q=Internet+video-+How+to+set+and+achieve+any+goal+you+have+in+your+life+by+John+Assaraf&src=IE-TopResult&FORM=IETR02&conversationid=&adlt=strict - (Accessed 5 October, 2017).

12. Jack Engelhard: Indecent Proposal film – https://en.wikipedia.org/wiki/Indecent_Proposal – (Accessed 5 October, 2017).

13. Jack Engelhard: Indecent Proposal film + https://www.moviefone.com/movie/indecent-proposal/7946/main/ – (Accessed 5 October, 2017).

14. Bellver Castle – http://www.northsouthguides.com/mallorca_bellver_castle.html - (Accessed 5 October, 2017).

15. Bellver Castle – https://www.triphistoric.com/castell-de-bellver-1001/ – (Accessed 5 October, 2017).

16. Serra de Tramuntana – https://en.wikipedia.org/wiki/Serra_de_Tramuntana – (Accessed 5 October, 2017).

17. Serra de Tramuntana – https://www.spain-holiday. com/Majorca/articles/discovering-mallorca-the-serra-de-tramuntana-mountains – (Accessed 5 October, 2017).

18. Serra de Tramuntana mountains – https://www. enjoymallorca.com/the-serra-de-tramuntana-mountains/ – (Accessed 5 October, 2017)

All scriptural references in this book were taken from the King James Version, and are in italics, except where indicated.

FOR INFORMATION, ENQUIRIES, OR BOOKINGS TO SPEAK

Please send all correspondence directly to:
Email: mikenwaduba@gmail.com

OTHER BOOKS WRITTEN BY THE AUTHOR

1. A Simple Guide for Bible Study
2. Questions and Answers on Tithes: Covenant of Prosperity
3. Amazing Grace in Abundance
4. Healing Balm for the Soul
5. The Holy Spirit and Supernatural Power
6. Mr and Mrs McGregor's Honeymoon on the Island of Santorini, Greece

To order the above books log into: *www.Amazon.co.uk*

ABOUT THE AUTHOR

Michael Nwaduba is a Minister of God with a calling to write and evangelise. Prior to God's calling into the ministry, he obtained qualifications in Business Administration, and Accountancy. He worked for nearly two decades as a finance officer for various establishments including being a Church Administrator for a Pentecostal Church in London.

He teaches the truth in the Word of God with a passion. He firmly believes in the integrity of the Word of God. You will find his books interesting and easy to understand because of the simple style he adopts as an author. You will also find biblical and practical life examples in his books.

Minister Mike is also a lawyer. He obtained his LLB (Hons) Law degree from London South Bank University, London, United Kingdom. He is a member of RCCG Victory House, London, and the former Personal Assistant (PA) to Pastor Leke Sanusi, Continental Overseer, RCCG Europe, and Special Assistant to The General Overseer (SATGO).